Bristol Bay Area Map

DEEP LIES
By
R. A. Quinn

(A Jacob Rohn Novel - Volume 2)

Deep Lies
Copyright ©2013 by R. A. Quinn

Deep Lies is a work of fiction. Names, characters, places and incidents are either the product of the author's imagination or are used fictitiously. Any resemblance to actual persons, living or dead, or to actual events or locales is entirely coincidental.

Published by:
Tier 1 Publishing
Pueblo, Colorado 81006

Revised 8/10/13

eBook version available
on Amazon and Barnes & Noble

Print version ISBN numbers:
ISBN-13: 978-0-9897332-0-5
ISBN-10: 0989733203

Table of Contents

Dedication

For Hans and Kevin

Acknowledgements

For everyone who has encouraged me to keep at this, thank you.

Thanks so much to the most patient and thorough proofreaders; Ron, Sean, Cindy, Papa and Chris.

For my patient and loving wife – your gentle support is indescribable. (A boot to the backside comes to mind.)

Chapter 1

Martin Folger had never been so happy; he was living his lifelong dream. At sixty-two years of age he had finally made the fishing trip of a lifetime. He traveled to Alaska and fished for a couple of weeks throughout Bristol Bay for three species of salmon, as well as for char, grayling, pike and his favorite fish of all time - monster sized rainbow trout. Not only had he been relishing the exceptional fishing, he had also camped, hiked and enjoyed the wilderness and local customs to their fullest in a region rich with tradition.

At the moment, Folger was fishing along the Kvichak River a couple of miles from Igiugig, Alaska, which is a small community located on the south edge of Lake Iliamna. The fishing was hot and he was reveling in the glory of standing knee deep in that wild Alaskan river with each plump trout he caught and released. There were many things that made his trip as special as it was but to be catching fish using flies he'd tied himself and a fly rod he'd built with his own hands made the moment even more magical.

'The guys back home will never believe all the stories I have to tell them.'

The day was warm as it was mid-summer. The sky was blue and there was just enough of a breeze to keep the bugs at bay. Folger had enjoyed the clean and fresh air since the first day when he arrived in Alaska and the current day was no different from all the others. The meandering river was clear and cold, perfect for fly fishing. The bed of the river was mostly sand with some rock and the high watermark all around told him that at certain times of the year, the river held much more water than it did at the present moment. There wasn't a soul in sight, just the way he preferred.

Several months earlier, Folger had decided it was time to travel to Alaska, albeit alone. The time he had spent fishing and sightseeing was incredible. He'd spent most of his adulthood dreaming of fishing in the wilderness of Alaska. So far he couldn't have been more pleased with what he had experienced and accomplished on his trip. Over the last few weeks he had seen more eagles than he could count, not to mention bear, moose, fox and enough fish to fill a good sized swimming pool.

He was set to begin the last leg of his journey; the finale of a spectacular fireworks display so to speak. If the first part of his trip had been the main course then the next few days were going to be the highly anticipated dessert. To Folger, it was going to be the ideal ending to the perfect journey.

The following day he was scheduled to catch a short flight across Lake Iliamna to the small rural town of the lake's namesake, Iliamna. Then he would catch another flight to Anchorage and after that a final flight to Valdez, Alaska, where he had lined up an overnight silver salmon and halibut fishing charter he intended to enjoy before returning home to Michigan. He could already envision the photo that would be taken of him standing next to a two-hundred pound halibut and several silver salmon. He had literally worn out numerous fishing magazines reading fishing stories and gazing at photographs of other lucky anglers who'd posed for such pictures as he was imagining. He had no idea how lucky, or unlucky, he actually was. Folger was a one in a million long shot to become just another tragic statistic.

Folger was lost in thought of how great it was going to be to recount each cast he had made, to recall each fish he had hooked and landed. He was so caught up in what he was doing and how each memory he had made would be replayed again and again that he didn't notice that there actually was another soul close by, watching him, waiting for him to exit the river and climb up onto the bank and enter the thick spruce and willows lining the river's edge.

After more than thirty minutes of watching the fly fisherman, the dark figure had his own wish come true. The angler turned and walked toward the bank of the swift river; he could hear the sloshing of the water as the wader clad fisherman made his way to the edge of the river and then scrambled up the bank. The fisherman entered the tree line and unknowingly continued straight toward him.

As Folger made his way around a clump of spruce trees, the concealed assailant made his move and quickly had control of his prey. The last thing that Martin Folger felt was the muscular arms of an unknown attacker encircle his neck. The last thought that went through Martin Folger's mind was how much he loved his wife. The strong and powerful assailant skillfully snapped Folger's neck, killing him instantly.

Chapter 2

"I do!" I said to answer the minister's question.

All the guests in the small chapel just outside of Wasilla, Alaska, were probably wondering why I paused briefly just before proudly saying those two words. I was actually thinking of jumping up in the air and clicking my heels together and shouting at the top of my lungs, *'You're damn straight I take this beautiful and loving woman as my wife – hell yes!'*

Okay, I settled on the traditional and direct *'I do'* instead. On the inside I was jumping up and down while clicking my heels together!

I could scarcely believe that this had come true for Whitney and me. Less than a year ago I was like a robot trudging through life with nothing to really look forward to. My job was good but I was bored. I had no one special in my life until I met an angel by the name of Whitney Cartwright.

Now Whitney and I are married. I still can't believe this has really happened for us.

I'd begun my law enforcement career in Colorado Springs after ending my tour in the military. I moved to Alaska after my fiancée had been killed in a car crash in Colorado. That was more than five years ago.

Working as a criminal investigator in Alaska was a good job and I firmly believed law enforcement had been my calling. There was nothing else I would ever want to do or could even imagine myself trying to accomplish.

The special investigative office under the State Attorney General where I worked was a great place to be, less politics and great cases. This particular unit was in the process of being formed when I was hired as one of the original investigators. We conduct criminal investigations, review cases or help with high profile cases around the state. On occasion we are called upon to conduct training for young officers new to the field. Wherever we're needed or directed to go by the state AG, that's where we go. Whitney understands the demands of my job and though I know she worries about the dangers inherent in being a cop, she supports me completely. I loved her beyond description.

"I now pronounce you man and wife; you may kiss the bride," said the minister as he closed his bible – what a cliché!

I lifted the thin white veil covering Whitney's face. Her eyes were big and wide in addition to being moist with tears. I pulled her close to me and kissed her soft lips. When I felt her respond, my heart shuttered and my knees weakened. For a moment I forgot all about the small crowd of friends and family who had filled the tiny chapel to witness our wedding. All that mattered was the woman who was in my arms. I'd never been happier or more complete in my entire life.

The guests slowly navigated their way through the reception line before leaving the church. There were hugs and handshakes and everyone was cheerful. I don't believe anyone had a smile that could match what was happening across my face at the time. I wished my parents had been alive to be part of this. Seeing how Whitney's mom and dad were glowing was absolutely remarkable.

After the church cleared, the entire wedding party had to stay an extra thirty minutes to finish the picture taking ritual. Afterwards, we made the short drive over to where the reception was being held and commenced to mingle with the guests.

"I knew this marriage was inevitable. I recall the day you went for coffee and afterwards you couldn't stop talking about the young lady who waited on you, and the ironic part is that you don't even like coffee," said my boss, Mark Dillon, as he slapped me on the back and erupted in laughter.

The one time in my life drawing the short straw was a good thing. I had to make the coffee run while we were waiting to testify in court and the rest is history so to speak.

Working for Mark Dillon was enjoyable. He was the sort of man who would fight for what was best for all who worked for him. I'd asked him to stand up for me at my wedding and he gladly accepted.

"Do you have a crystal ball Mark?" I mockingly asked.

"As a matter of fact I do," was Mark's quick comeback.

"So tell me, when are you meeting that special lady yourself?" I pointedly asked.

"Been there and done that my friend. I have the scars on my heart and my financial future to prove it," Mark quickly answered as if he'd already had this same conversation prior to now and his dialogue was already planned out.

Seeing that this could be a very sore subject, I changed the direction of the conversation. "How are you going to handle things without me for two weeks while Whitney and I take off for some fun, travels and high adventure?"

We were scheduled to fly to Dillingham the following day. Located at the northern edge of Bristol Bay in south central Alaska, Dillingham served as a major hub for commercial fishermen, hunters, anglers and tourists who traveled to the region.

"Let's see, I was sort of hoping that the world would put all crime on hold, at least in Alaska, while you're away. I have my doubts whether we could function without your expertise." Mark sarcastically said with a straight face.

"Okay smart ass, I don't wish bad things on anyone but I hope you have to eat your words and when you call me for help I'll put you on ignore," I retorted.

Mark quickly drained his glass as a waiter passed with a tray of fresh drinks. He skillfully exchanged his empty glass for two full ones. "You two have the time of your lives down in Bristol Bay camping and fishing. Don't worry about us chumps up here busting our butts day in and day out."

"No worries there, I've already forgotten who you are. Who are you anyway and why are you at my wedding?" I asked with a sarcastic smirk of my own.

"Who's the smart ass now?" Mark shot back as he placed an empty glass on the corner of a nearby table.

All the while, I was watching Whitney as she gracefully moved about the room. I was astounded at her charm and the warm smile she had for everyone there.

My head was beginning to feel the copious amounts of champagne I'd consumed. Everyone wanted to slap me on the back and have their own special toast with me. There was no way I would turn anyone down, not a toast, good drink or friendship.

We finally were seated and had some food which helped the lightheadedness I was feeling. There were dances and more toasts and a few speeches but I lost count. It was a fantastic reception. There were many cards and some gifts which Whitney and I opened and I was certain we said 'thank you' about twenty-five thousand times.

It was getting late and most of the guests had left. Whitney's parents and most of the wedding party were all that remained. I was full of food and drink but at least my head was clearing up. Whitney was still flushed from the warmth of the room and the champagne she had consumed.

Just as we were about to say our goodbyes and go back to our place - I liked the sound of calling our home 'our place' - a waiter approached me with a white envelope and a small white box about four inches square with a blue bow tied around it.

"Mr. Rohn, this had fallen behind the table where the gifts had been. I apologize for the mishap but I brought it right to you when it was found as we were cleaning," the waiter said shyly.

"Thank you; it's fine," I said as the waiter hurried away.

The white envelope and small box had J. Rohn printed on them with a black marker. I opened the envelope which had a card which read: *"I wasn't sure what to get you but maybe this will do. M."*

I opened the small package and viewed its contents. It took a moment for what I was looking at to sink into my alcohol soaked brain and for me to realize what I was seeing. I quickly replaced the top on the box. I was hoping no one had seen me turn as white as a sheet. What in the hell! If I hadn't already sobered up, I was certainly completely sober now.

Chapter 3

Several days earlier, Chuck Jones settled back into the first class seat of the Alaska Airlines aircraft that was about to take off from San Diego, California, and fly to Seattle, Washington. From there he would catch a connecting flight that would take him to 'The Land of the Midnight Sun' – Alaska. In his twenty plus years of this work he'd never been to Alaska. After this job that would no longer be true. To fly on Alaska Airlines was both ironic and funny to him for some reason.

It had been as simple as always. He received an email that came to him after it had bounced off at least two dozen servers worldwide – impossible to trace according to the techno geek he paid to set it up. He was provided with the basic details of the job he was being hired to do. He emailed a bank code to the employer along with instructions to deposit half of the one-hundred and fifty thousand dollars this job would pay him.

Once the deposit was made, he requested the full details of the job and the subject of the hit. Chuck Jones was a gun for hire with at least fifty kills to his credit. He was precise, effective, and ruthless. In the dark underworld in which he lived and survived, he was considered one of the best at what he did.

Chuck Jones was just one of the many aliases that he used while working on a contract. For this particular trip, he was posing as an avid outdoorsman traveling to Alaska with plans of fishing for king salmon and other trophy fish and then in the early fall he would change gears and begin a hunt for moose and bear.

That was his cover story anyway. At least it was partly true; he'd be hunting after all. Jones smiled at his sadistic humor. His cunning ways made him untouchable. He was now, as always, on top of his game. The great part of it was that he in fact was an avid big game hunter and fisherman. This was like a paid vacation to him.

He could give a shit less about who hired him or who he had to hit. As long as the money was good and he had information enough to do the job right, it was pretty much all the same to him. He was confident that in the past he had been hired for similar jobs by the mob, drug cartels and even the U.S. Government though he couldn't prove it. Still, he didn't really care as long as he was paid and he normally demanded and received a handsome salary.

He was pretty sure this job came from someone in Denver, Colorado, even though it didn't actually matter. It was something the employer had said in their correspondence that gave it away. Whoever it was that hired him was a bit careless but that didn't matter at all. Not a living soul knew who he was, or what he looked like. He'd learned to keep his identity secret and the millions he has amassed over the years had been calling out to him louder and louder each day to retire in the lap of luxury. Perhaps this will be his last job and he will put into action the meticulous plans he has made to disappear for the rest of his natural life.

The target for this job was a man named Jacob Rohn. Some pain in the ass criminal investigator in Alaska who lives in Anchorage. He'd done his usual background on the guy. Seemed like small potatoes to him but he must have stepped on somebody's toe pretty hard for the money being paid for a seemingly simple job. He didn't have anything against cops in general; he thought they were a lot like him, just on different sides is all. It won't be the first cop he'd taken out and probably won't be his last.

The cabin lights were turned down after the attending staff made their required announcements. The roar of the powerful engines filled his ears as the jet slowly lifted off the ground. He could hear the whir of the flaps being moved and felt the jolt of the landing gear as they folded up neatly into their compartments under the plane.

Before drifting off into a peaceful sleep, Jones's last thought was wondering how in the hell something as huge as the airliner he was in could so easily take off and fly in the night sky. Incredible!

Upon arriving in Anchorage, Alaska; Jones rented a car and found an average hotel that took his two week reservation and cash payment without question. He'd been following Jacob Rohn for a few days now and had pretty much learned all he needed to know. Rohn was being married that very day to a striking young woman. She would lose her new husband no sooner than they were married but she was safe in his mind. He didn't kill for free and certainly didn't kill for the sake of killing. It was time to put his plan into action, get the job accomplished and move on.

Chapter 4

"Guy business," is what I told Whitney as I took a hold of Mark and literally dragged him to a small room void of any staff or wedding party.

"Look at this note card."

Mark had a puzzled look on his face but he took the card and read it. "That's nice. What? Did someone give you a tie you want to return or something?"

"No, it's far beyond a cheesy wedding gift," I said as I handed him the small box. "This was what came with the card and they both are addressed to me."

Just like a child being made to eat his vegetables, Mark took the box from me with pained hesitation. He opened it and looked inside. "What the...?"

Mark looked up at me with great concern etched all over his face, the apathy present there just moments before having been completely evaporated.

In the box nestled in cotton was a .44 handgun round. On the side of the brass casing written in black was 'J. Rohn.'

"Are you fucking kidding me?" exclaimed Mark. "A bullet with your name on it from M . . . Marcus?" You could see the lights flickering and then come on full force in Mark's expression.

Marcus: we've heard that name before. A few months ago while working on a double homicide case in the small community of Fort Yukon, there was a player in that whole mess identified only as Marcus who we were certain had been the brains behind a drug smuggling operation into Alaska and a double murder. All we were convinced of was that Marcus was most likely in Denver, Colorado. No agency could identify Marcus. We had a single name that couldn't be connected to anyone. Marcus did a first-rate job of hiding his identity from the feds and the Colorado authorities. Our investigation alone cost him thousands of dollars in seized drugs in addition to spoiling a budding enterprise. He undoubtedly would have a reason to hate me enough to want me dead.

My head had completely cleared. "This was among the gifts we were given at the reception. It had fallen off the table and a waiter just brought it to me. I've no idea when this got here or who may have brought it," I said.

Mark was all business now. "Okay," he began. "Was there anyone at the wedding or reception you didn't know? I didn't notice anyone I wasn't familiar with even if I didn't know them personally."

"No, we kept it small and simple. I knew everyone there."

Mark's face was tightening up. I could tell he had something on his mind.

"You know Jake, dealers like Marcus lose drug shipments all the time; why do you suppose this fucker would have such a hard on for you? Do you think there's any chance you crossed this asshole before? I mean back when you were a cop in Colorado Springs."

"Since I first heard of this shithead a few months ago I've wondered if there was something in my past connecting me to him or if there was a chance I dealt with him in Colorado when I worked there but I just can't recall anything. I'm positive I never dealt with anyone named Marcus. I've called and spoken with some of my old partners and they've drawn a blank too."

"Have you told Whitney about this?" asked Mark.

No doubt I gave Mark one of those looks that spoke volumes.

"Tell Whitney! Are you crazy? Tell the woman I just married that on her wedding day I get a threat on my life!"

Mark and I stood in silence for several seconds. My thoughts were racing out of control much like a fully loaded truck careening wildly down a mountain side without any brakes. I had to slow things down and begin thinking rationally. I was the first to break the awkward silence.

"I have to continue as if everything was normal. There's no reason to alarm Whitney or anyone else. The thing to do is keep my guard up and look for anything out of the ordinary and be ready all the time."

Mark was shaking his head in agreement. "I know a retired fed who lives here in Anchorage. He used to do some undercover work and has some training in covert operations from my recollection of speaking with him. I also have some funds available that would allow him to travel along with you and watch your back. You have to agree with this or else you'll force me to put my foot down and not allow you to leave my sight."

"Okay Mark, that sounds good. I'll agree but he'll have to do this without Whitney knowing."

"Done," said Mark.

"Can you have your friend meet with us at our office before noon tomorrow?"

"I'm certain he'll be up to helping us as long as he's available," Mark said.

"Let's plan on meeting at 10:00 a.m. then. You know that if Marcus is watching me, he could be ready to make his move now," I added.

"We'll wait until everyone leaves and I'll follow you and Whitney from a distance to make sure you get home okay. We can review the plan when we meet in the morning. In the meantime I'll get the names of all the wait staff and caterer and check them out. Let's see if we can find out how that gift and card made its way to the reception, which could give us more to go on."

Mark was like a brother to me. I trusted his judgment completely.

"Sounds good, thanks Mark."

That's exactly what happened. By the time Mark and I returned, Whitney and her parents were all that remained in the reception hall. After a few more hugs and pleasantries, her parents left and so did Whitney and I. The drive to our place was uneventful, with one eye on Whitney and the other on the rearview mirror.

At a plush home in Denver, Colorado, a smallish man they called Marcus was reading a text message.

"Everything's a go; I expect the problem to be fixed soon. I'll be in touch."

Marcus tossed his phone up onto a small bar where he was seated in his home and was deep in thought. A wry grin made its way across Marcus's face.

'Rohn is getting married today. I hope he enjoys the short relationship. Maybe sending him that gift was being too cocky. Maybe I should've told Jones that I did it; Rohn will be expecting something now. Maybe I just hate Rohn so much I want him to suffer some before his life is over. Oh well, hindsight is 20/20 as they say. Maybe, no, not maybe, I just don't give a shit; he's cost me for the last time and if Jones is as good as he is rumored to be, it doesn't matter what Rohn knows or does for that matter.'

Marcus used a remote control to click on the T.V. as he sat back onto a leather sofa and closed his eyes.

Jones immediately felt something had changed. Rohn looked cautious as he left the reception hall. He'd been following Rohn on and off for a few days and now, on his wedding night, Rohn has changed his posture to be more vigilant. Rohn knows something isn't right.

This was an example of how important his ability to accurately read situations and people was to his health and wellbeing. Using this finely tuned skill had saved his life on more than one occasion over the past twenty years. Jones knew it was best to back off and evaluate these new set of circumstances before he continued with this job. Making contact with his employer had now become necessary. Something about this entire situation was causing a sick feeling in his stomach. He wasn't accustomed to such an emotion and he certainly didn't like it.

Chapter 5

Our wedding night was pretty much what I expected. Well, I didn't anticipate being worried that at any minute someone was going to bust through the front door and mow us down with an automatic weapon of some sort. That had a way of somewhat dampening the moment. I was able to play it off with Whitney by telling her that all the alcohol, excitement and long day had taken a huge toll on me. There was a lot of truth to that; getting older was plain hell.

I'm not saying the night was a flop by any means; in fact we were awesome together. The first night as husband and wife was a night to remember.

As Whitney and I finished up a quick breakfast, I told her that I had to meet Mark at the office just to ensure everything I usually handled was taken care of in my absence. While I was gone she could check that we had everything packed and we would catch our flight to Dillingham later that afternoon.

I made the fifteen minute drive to our offices and was inside by 9:30 a.m. As I entered into the main conference room I immediately saw Mark Dillon and a man I'd never met.

Mark made the introduction as I entered the room. "Jake, this is Glenn Baxter. I spoke about him last night. Glenn is available and eager to help."

I noted Glenn had a firm grip when we shook hands. He stood to greet me which spoke volumes about the man. Glenn was about 5'10" tall and had short white hair cut in a crew cut style and I guessed he was maybe sixty-five years old. His skin was tanned and leathery in appearance. He didn't get suntanned as he was by living in Anchorage. Glenn had a strong jaw and good smile. I liked him at once and felt he was capable and trustworthy. If Mark knew him and believed in his ability to watch my back, that was good enough for me.

"Glenn and I have been talking and he feels confident that if there's anyone following you he can spot them without being noticed," said Mark.

"I've received and provided training in undercover operations and worked some specific details quite similar to this particular assignment. I've known Mark a long time and I'm willing to see this to the end," added Glenn.

"We've discussed this and though Glenn will be armed, he's only there to observe and report anything that he feels is suspicious in order to prevent an attempt on your life Jake."

I was glad that Mark and Glenn had talked this through but it was my life they were talking about. "Just so that I understand it better, Glenn, you will follow my wife and I at a distance with the luxury of knowing where we're going and keep me apprised of any potential threat you may spot?" I asked.

Glenn sat up a bit straighter in his chair and answered my question. "Yeah, generally you and I can communicate by text message but I realize the Bristol Bay area is remote and communications can be unreliable. However, that same remoteness will work in our favor as it should be simpler to spot anyone who is following your movements."

"Sounds like a good plan to me Mark. Who else knows about this arrangement?"

Mark had an uncomfortable look about him. "I don't think I want anyone to know about this but us three. Are we all good with that? After all, we're not completely positive there's an actual threat out there."

I spoke up first, "I'm good with it."

"So am I," said Glenn.

"Oh and Jake, we checked out everyone who worked at your reception and we came up with nothing. No one could recall who brought in that card and gift or even when it showed up. I suspect Marcus simply paid someone to drop it off and it was done without anyone paying any attention or noticing anything out of the ordinary. In addition, the card, bullet and box that it came in have been checked over by lab personnel and the only latent prints were yours, mine and the waiter's. It's being tested for DNA but our hopes for any positive results are slim at best. Unlike what's implied by television shows, DNA test results aren't available in a short time; we're looking at weeks before we get any information back."

"That creepy bastard has a way of making himself invisible and untouchable," I said.

"Then it's settled. Glenn, you have Jake's flight schedule and contact information. Let's see if we can find out who may be targeting Jake. Hopefully there's no one and all this turns out to be is a sick prank," said Mark.

"Mark, maybe you can re-visit the case from up North and follow-up with authorities in Colorado and the DEA; perhaps this Marcus shithead has popped up on someone's radar, you never know," I suggested.

"Already on it Jake. I placed some calls this morning and Glenn even had a few ideas on how to put out some feelers and I've done that as well. So far we have nothing back."

"Well then, I guess all that's left now is to go on a honeymoon. I only wish I had the guts to tell Whitney about this but I just don't see the upside to that. She'll want to go anyway and both of us will be worried sick. At least this way it will be only me who's concerned and anxious about this the entire time."

No one knew what to say to that. This particular situation was secret service and dignitary protection kind of shit that I was unfamiliar with. I wasn't completely certain on how to best proceed or what the right answer was. Getting a threat on your life isn't an everyday thing. Were we supposed to hide under a rock or something?

"Okay, done. Whitney and I have a plane to catch. Glenn, I hope you have your bug dope packed because you're gonna need it and if you plan on fishing, I bet you a bottle of Jack Daniels here and now that I catch the biggest as well as the most fish."

Glenn smiled at that. "I'll take that bet, only make mine Crown!"

With that I shook Glenn and Mark's hand and headed for the door.

Chapter 6

Chuck Jones sat in his hotel room near Ted Stevens Anchorage International Airport. He'd survived all these years by being meticulous in his planning and careful beyond description. Time was on his side and what he saw last night was a perfect example of an instance in his business when it was healthy to take a step back and evaluate his plan and make the correct adjustments.

He saw Jake Rohn exit that reception hall and all of a sudden his head was on a swivel. It was odd enough that the bride and groom were among the last to leave but seeing Rohn looking around as he was had him spooked. Then, within a minute or less, he saw Mark Dillon exit the reception hall and he too looked as if he was searching for something or someone before entering his car and following along behind Rohn.

Yep, something had happened between the time they arrived at the reception and the moment they left. The question is what could've occurred that made these two professional cops become so paranoid on an occasion when they should've been loose and carefree. In fear of being detected, he remained in his hiding spot for nearly two hours before returning to his vehicle parked nearly a half mile away.

He couldn't come up with any logical solution but he had to figure things out before he proceeded any further. He didn't want to get within a mile of Rohn until he had some answers.

Going against his instincts but knowing it was his only move, he picked up one of his pay as you go cell phones and dialed the number his employer provided in the event there was a need for direct contact. Jones felt that there was a need.

"Hello," said Marcus who picked up his phone after about three rings. He recognized the number as that of the man he sent to Alaska.

"What in God's name is going on? Rohn knows something is up," said Jones into the phone.

Marcus thought he was going to laugh out loud. The caller was disguising his voice with something that made him sound like a cross between Donald Duck and Porky Pig. *'This guy was serious, crazy or both,'* Marcus thought.

"Are you there?" asked Jones.

"I'm here."

"What's going on with Rohn? He knows something isn't right; all of a sudden he began acting like I would act if I knew someone was after me," Jones said.

"Look, I did something that you're not gonna like but I did it anyway."

Marcus went on to explain that when he learned of Rohn's wedding he sent him a gift: a bullet with Rohn's name on it that he'd paid one of his connections to have delivered to the reception. He said how his hatred for Rohn had gotten the better of him.

There was dead silence on the phone after Marcus finished his explanation. He was scared as to how this man would react.

Jones began slowly. Even though he was furious, his demeanor was calm. "You've jeopardized this mission but more importantly, my safety. I've no desire to chase this man to Dillingham. As of now, I'm no longer employed by you. Goodbye!"

"Wait!" Marcus all but screamed into the phone. "I know I messed up, but you have to know how bad I want this man dead. He's plagued me for years and has literally cost me millions. I'll double your fee, just tell me where to send the rest of the original one-hundred and fifty thousand and at the conclusion of the job I'll pay you an additional one-hundred and fifty thousand plus an extra twenty-five thousand for expenses. I know this will take much longer because of what I did but I'm offering a total of three-hundred and twenty-five thousand for the job."

There was dead silence on the phone but Marcus knew the killer was considering his new offer since he hadn't disconnected – god, all people were the same, greedy beyond description!

After maybe thirty seconds more of silence Jones spoke. "I'll think this through and give you my answer within twelve hours. If you haven't heard from me by then, you can kiss me and your down payment goodbye."

At that, the phone connection went dead. Marcus grinned like a fat kid who'd just eaten the plate of cookies his mom had made for her bridge club, not caring what the consequences would be should he be caught.

After disconnecting with his employer, Jones thought about the sweetened pot and how the plan would have to change after his boss's indiscretion. He was good enough to outwit some goofy cop for crying out loud. He'd already been considering retirement and the money he would make off of this job alone would push him beyond his planned portfolio needs.

Jones came to his decision rather quickly but waited over an hour to send an email to his employer. *"I've decided to complete this contract as long as my conditions are met. The fee is now half a million, total, with half of it due before I continue. If you want this job completed, and judging by your desire to see it through, that's the price and isn't negotiable. You've already paid me seventy-five thousand, so you must pay me an additional one-hundred seventy-five thousand up front; deposited in the same account as before. Upon completion, you will pay me the remaining quarter of a million dollars. As soon as I verify that the money requested has been deposited, I'll carry on and notify you once the contract has been completed."*

Jones looked over the email, felt it was sufficient and clicked on the send button. It was less than fifteen minutes before he got the reply he expected: *"Agreed!"*

The hired gunman sat back and smiled. *'Shit, I should've asked for a million.'* It was time to pack and catch a flight to Dillingham.

Chapter 7

The Pen Air Saab 340 turboprop aircraft rolled to a stop on the parking apron of the Dillingham airport. The pilot shut down both engines and after the propeller blades came to a complete standstill, the ground crew wheeled a set of stairs up to the exit doorway and opened it up. Whitney had an anxious smile on her face as she prepared to exit the plane. She'd lived in Alaska all her life but had done very little camping or fishing. Since being with me she discovered that she liked them both. This trip was something we both wanted and needed. Whitney didn't know yet but I'd made some preliminary arrangements for us to take that exotic honeymoon most couples go on. The plan was for us to go this December. The Hawaiian Island of Maui awaits Mr. and Mrs. Jacob Rohn. That'll have to wait its turn however. Who wants to leave Alaska in the summer months anyway? After you spend all winter in some miserable cold weather, your reward is to play in the warm sunshine that covers Alaska in the summer.

Dillingham is situated along Nushagak Bay at the confluence of the Nushagak and Wood Rivers, an inlet of Bristol Bay, in southwestern Alaska. The population is approximately 2,200 but I'm certain that number rises substantially during the commercial fishing season as well as the sport fishing and hunting months.

Commercial fishing remains an important part of the local economy. The Alaska salmon fishery is one of the only certified sustainable wild salmon fisheries left in the world and Dillingham plays an important role in the Bristol Bay fishery.

Our plans included meeting up with a Village Public Safety Officer or VPSO as they are generally called by the locals. First Sergeant Blaine Alexander works out of Dillingham and travels about the region to help other VPSOs with training and case investigations. I met Blaine a few years back and though only rarely have the two of us worked together, we've attended some of the same training sessions on occasion and he always invites me to travel to Dillingham and go fishing with him. I've traveled to Dillingham in the past and spent time with him and his family which was enjoyable.

Blaine is Yupik Alaskan Native and of course knows the local culture and believes strongly in keeping not only his own community but all of Alaska's rural communities safe. He's a fair man, an intelligent man and certainly a wise man. He's dedicated himself to a profession that's so often disliked by the residents of the communities he protects and is always subject to intense scrutiny.

The VPSO program began in the seventies as a program to provide public safety officers to rural Alaskan villages. In the early eighties the program turned into what it is today as a statewide project that is overseen by the Alaska State Troopers. The VPSOs are employed by regional non-profit organizations but are trained and supervised by state troopers stationed in hub communities around the state. VPSOs are stationed throughout the rural regions and are trained as first responders in law enforcement, fire safety, search and rescue and of course first aid. The VPSO in most communities is the go-to person for anything public safety related and is generally the only public safety presence in most villages.

My hat is off to these men and women who undertake a VPSO position. Most are from the area where they are hired to work and ultimately have to take enforcement actions involving family or life-long friends. There have been many debates over the matter but at the present time these public safety officers work unarmed and always have.

As first responders, the VPSOs are the eyes and ears of the Alaska State Troopers who don't possess sufficient numbers to have a constant presence in every Alaska community. VPSOs conduct misdemeanor case investigations but call upon the troopers for assistance with felony cases.

As I exited the plane I couldn't help but wonder if someone who was on this plane was watching me. I certainly was paying attention but didn't want to seem paranoid. I didn't see Glenn Baxter on the aircraft and thought he must have travelled out on an earlier flight. It was 7:30 p.m. by the time we made it into the terminal and retrieved our bags.

My earlier thought must have been right on the money. I saw Baxter blending in as a worker at the airport by doing some janitorial work. Just as we were about to exit the baggage claim area and go out into the parking lot, I noticed a familiar face coming through the double doors.

"Blaine, it's so good to see you," I approached Blaine and we 'man hugged' for a moment and then backed away and shook hands. "Blaine, let me introduce Mrs. Jacob Rohn, this is Whitney Cartwright, I mean Rohn."

Whitney was fairly shy but she stepped up and greeted Blaine. "So very nice to finally meet you; Jacob has told me so much about you."

Blaine was all smiles and very gracious. "It's good to meet you as well; let's go you two, dinner is waiting for us."

We loaded our bags into Blaine's pickup and made the five minute drive to his house which faced Nushagak Bay on the edge of Dillingham's city limit.

Blaine and I got our bags inside the house where we were met by his wife, Diane. Whitney and Diane had already introduced themselves to each other and were talking away like long lost friends. It was always so wonderful to see Whitney warm up to strangers so easily. If only the entire world was that friendly.

After polishing off my second helping of moose roast, potatoes and carrots I had to push my plate back. "Diane, the food was perfect! Thank you so much for taking care of us."

Diane beamed at the compliment. "Jake, if you bring me some fish I'll smoke them before you leave. But if not, I have plenty you can take back with you to Anchorage."

"Are you saying you doubt my ability to catch fish?" I reply.

"No, what I'm saying is I doubt you'll have the opportunity to catch fish," at that Diane winked at Whitney.

We all laughed.

"Blaine, can I talk to you privately for a few minutes?" I asked. "Sorry ladies, but you know how business can be at times."

"Sure thing," Blaine said as he stood and motioned for me to follow him.

We went into a small office and Blaine closed the door.

"What is it Jake?"

"There's something I want you to know but you have to promise me that you'll keep it to yourself."

"Okay, no problem," Blaine assured me.

I told Blaine about the threatening gift and the mysterious Marcus. I also let him know that Glenn Baxter was in town and that he was there to identify any potential threat to my safety, if there actually was a threat. I showed Blaine a picture of Baxter that I'd taken with my phone.

It was good to have Blaine keeping an eye out too. After all who would recognize a stranger in town quicker than him? With Blaine's permission I took a photo of him with my phone and sent it to Baxter by way of a text message. I also felt that Blaine needed to know that there may be a level of danger with me being at his home if this threat was indeed real.

"Jake, I'd be hurt if you and Whitney were to stay somewhere other than with us. I have the best damn alarm system available with that Rotty - Saint Bernard mix out there keepin' an eye on things. He's the best dog; Rufus is both friendly and gentle but he has the protective instincts to keep us safe."

"Thanks Blaine. I was certain I could count on you but I had to let you know. With the decision to keep this under wraps, you're the only other person in town who knows about this."

"So, are you and Whitney still going fishing and camping as planned?" Blaine asked me.

"We're flying out tomorrow and getting dropped off at a lake to the west for a couple days. After returning to Dillingham, we still plan on going to Aleknagik Lake for a few days. Is everything still a go for us to use your boat and cabin at the end of Aleknagik Lake?"

"Sure thing," said Blaine.

"Alright, it's a plan then," I said.

With that we re-joined the ladies in the front room. They'd already cleaned up the supper mess and were talking about sewing. I guess sewing is a universal language among women, kind of like guys talking about cars – it's an easy conversation.

"We have an early day tomorrow; you ready to call it a night?" I asked Whitney.

"Sure Jacob," said Whitney as she turned to face Blaine and Diane in order to address them. "Thank you two so much for the hospitality, Jacob has told me so many good things about you both."

Blaine and Diane both seemed to blush. I don't think they thought of taking us in and feeding us as an inconvenience; it was how they were. They both smiled at Whitney and let her know she was always welcome.

Whitney and I said our goodnights and headed off to bed. We both were tired and very excited about having our time alone over the next few days.

Chapter 8

Glenn Baxter made the hour long flight to Dillingham on a charter that Mark Dillon had arranged. He arrived long before Jake and Whitney were scheduled to. Baxter thought it was a good idea to get there and get into a position that would allow him to observe everyone who arrived at the small airport over the next couple of days.

Jake and Whitney would arrive early in the evening according to the schedule that had been provided by Rohn. They would be met by a VPSO who was stationed in Dillingham and the plan was for Rohn and his bride to spend the night at the VPSO's home. The couple was scheduled to fly out to a remote lake the following morning and be out of town for a few days. His plan was to watch all persons arriving by plane with hopes of spotting anyone following Rohn.

Dillingham was a fairly busy town this time of year. Alaska Airlines and Pen Air both made a few flights to the commercial fishing town each day. As for many of Alaska's remote communities, the only other way to get to Dillingham was by boat, and that would take a person several days or weeks to accomplish. There were no passenger services by boat anyway, so that route seemed unlikely. So a flight on one of the airlines was left as the most likely way anyone could arrive in town to follow Rohn.

Baxter had shown his badge and credentials to the airport manager and TSA supervisor and told them he was conducting surveillance just to identify a potential passenger who was a person of interest in an ongoing investigation and he would stay outside the security gates and simply observe persons who arrived. They had very few questions and after showing the letter of authorization Mark Dillon had provided, it was pretty straight forward and getting their blessing was easy enough.

Baxter disguised himself as a janitor and each time a flight arrived, he would busy himself emptying trash and sweeping in just the right areas so that he could see all the passengers who entered into the terminal once they had deplaned. With a good idea of what to look for, Baxter hoped he would spot the person who would arrive in town with the sole aim of killing Rohn.

It was probable that the person he sought would be alone. He might look as if he belonged there but not completely and act nonchalantly but seem to be paranoid about who may be following them. Baxter felt this was just the kind of mission he had trained for all those years as a federal officer.

By the time it was 5:00 in the afternoon, two flights had arrived but not a single passenger from either flight met his profile. All were either traveling in groups or had someone meeting them that seemed to be legitimate residents of the area. At about 5:15 p.m. the last Alaska Airline's flight of the day arrived. There were about forty-five passengers who exited that particular plane. Probably more than what had arrived on the two smaller planes combined.

Baxter thought that the terminal area he was cleaning for the third time had not seen such care since it was new. There were three passengers on that flight who fit the bill of what he was looking for. There was a woman who seemed to go out of her way to avoid people; she was alone and seemed like a fish out of water. It wouldn't be impossible or unheard of for the assassin he was seeking to be a female. She was forty-ish; she had two checked bags large enough to conceal a weapon that a sniper, or hit man in this instance, might use to make a hit.

The second man was about fifty. He was dressed like someone that intended on going hunting judging by his attire. He was alone also. He actually picked up two checked bags as well, one being definitely big enough to hold a weapon.

The last gentleman was a nerd if there ever was a nerd. Probably late thirties, white button up shirt and a bowtie. He was alone and actually had three checked bags and two were hard sided cases, certainly capable of housing weapons. If this was the guy, he tried too hard not to stick out because he couldn't have stuck out anymore if he had a red flag tied to his backside.

Of the three, he was fairly certain the woman wasn't who he was looking for. The nerd could've been the guy but the hunter just didn't act like a hunter. He didn't stop and look at the maps on the wall or the pictures of the fish and game taken by others. He also walked right by a stuffed grizzly bear at the front of the terminal without as much as a glance. He looked like a hunter but just didn't act like it.

Baxter had checked with TSA in Anchorage asking about any weapons being shipped to Dillingham on the day's flight. The agent actually laughed at him. There were numerous weapons going to Dillingham on the day's flights; just like every other day. There were so many that it was rare that they had passenger names – just the numbers. It was nearing hunting season after all.

Each of his three possible suspects called and caught a cab and left the airport property. Since there was only one cab company in town, finding these three would be easy enough. He needed to stick around for one more flight. That was Rohn's flight which happened to be the last flight of the day.

At 7:15 p.m., the last Pen Air flight rolled up and shut down. All the passengers exited the aircraft and came into the terminal. One by one Baxter was able to see and mentally dismiss each passenger as a possible suspect. None came close to the profile he was looking for. He saw Rohn and his bride; they both looked incredibly happy and very much into one another. If Rohn was distracted, he didn't show it.

After having the chance to get a look at the passengers from that last flight, Baxter took the state DOT truck that was parked for him in front of the airport and drove to the Bay View B&B Mark had booked for him. The place he chose was great. Each guest room was a standalone cabin that allowed for maximum privacy. Each cabin had a bedroom, bath and small kitchen area. Mark Dillon surely had some good contacts throughout Alaska. He would have to tell him thanks for these remarkable accommodations.

Baxter checked into the B&B and thought he would take a shower to cool off and get cleaned up before preparing his microwaveable meal. Upon exiting the shower he saw a glimpse of movement in the shadows of the already darkened room. In a flash an assailant was to the rear of Baxter and skillfully looped a garrote around his neck. Upon tightening the ligature, Glenn Baxter passed out and died quietly as his larynx was instantly crushed.

Chuck Jones let Baxter slide to the floor. He shook his head; he hated to kill for free but this was for self preservation. He felt quite fortunate that he recognized the older man who was cleaning in the airport when he arrived earlier in the day. He knew the man as Glenn Baxter, federal agent. He was certain Baxter wasn't spending his retirement years as a janitor at the airport in Dillingham, Alaska. When Jones was much younger, Baxter taught a portion of an undercover operations seminar that he'd attended. No doubt Baxter was there to spot him. Judging by what he found on Baxter's cell phone and how Baxter had acted, he didn't believe he'd been recognized or even suspected by Baxter.

In Anchorage, he befriended a group of sportsmen whose destination was a fishing lodge near Dillingham. When they deplaned, he followed them and blended in with their group. No one was the wiser. He spotted Baxter right off; as he would have been himself - Baxter was interested in loners and didn't give him a second glance.

Jones picked up the phone in the small room and dialed a few numbers. Once there was a voice on the other end Jones spoke. "This is cabin thirteen, I just checked in. I wanted you to know my plans have changed and I may stay a few days longer. I'll be keeping some odd hours so there's no need to have my room cleaned until I let you know otherwise. I'll be sure to stop by soon and settle up if there's any extra that I'll owe. Thank you so much."

Jones smiled as he set the phone back down on the table. *'How convenient! I'll take this state truck back to the airport and leave it there. I'll keep this cell phone too, who knows what I can learn from it before I discard it into the choppy waters of Bristol Bay. This federal ID and handgun of Baxter's may have some use as well.'*

Chapter 9

We woke to a beautiful and somewhat warm sunny morning in Dillingham; it was late enough in the summer and there were enough hours of darkness at night so that it was easy to rest. Alaska is a large state; at this time of the year Fairbanks only gets maybe two hours of darkness, but Dillingham is much farther south and therefore it does get more *'nighttime'*. I slept like a rock and felt more rested than I had in days. The fresh air carrying the slight fragrances from the murky water in the bay wasn't overpowering at all; it was soothing and crisp.

The birds were chirping in the already warm sunshine and I didn't believe there was a cloud in the sky. So often you hear people talk about how clear the night sky is in Alaska, and they are right. I think that the sky during the day is even more magnificent and when it's clear as it was on this day, the blue sky was sharp and more intense than I've ever seen. The tide was obviously out as the water had receded in the bay at least eighty to a hundred feet. Mud flats were visible where there had been water the evening before. The tides were certainly a factor for vessels of all sizes that traversed these waters. Seagulls by the hundreds could be seen picking at the now exposed floor of Bristol Bay.

Whitney was ready for our adventure to begin. It was 8:00 a.m. when we were dropped off at Shannon's Pond by Blaine. This was a small airstrip and floatplane base on the edge of Dillingham used primarily by small air taxi services and floatplane operations for both commercial and private needs. I let Blaine know it would be a couple of days before we returned but since I had a satellite phone among my gear, I would be able to let him know in advance when we would actually get back. On this trip, time wasn't a factor and we could stay away as long as we pleased.

I'd taken off and landed in a floatplane several times before now. This will be Whitney's first time in such a plane. Many people in the lower 48 would refer to these aircraft as seaplanes, but locally they were known as floatplanes. They're aircraft of varying sizes that have pontoons attached where the landing gear would normally be. The floats, as they are referred to, stabilize and hold the plane up on water during taxi and takeoff and are aerodynamic enough for the plane to maintain normal flight but may reduce the overall airspeed and payload some due to the size and weight of the floats. Planes with floats on them operate just like any other plane except that the takeoff and landings are on water, perfect for flying to remote locations as Whitney and I were about to undertake.

It was odd that I hadn't heard back from Glenn Baxter after I sent him that text last night but perhaps he slept in and had nothing to report anyway. Glenn knew what our schedule was and would wait in Dillingham until Whitney and I returned. We were perhaps being overly cautious anyway.

Our pilot, Bob Johnson, had just finished the safety briefing he was required to give us. I was ready to go … I was also sure I could hear the fish jumping from the backseat of that plane.

Bob seemed like a nice enough fellow and was definitely the quiet type. I had the opportunity to talk with him while we loaded our gear into the aircraft. He'd traveled to Alaska after a nasty divorce ten years earlier. Bob had worked in the Bristol Bay region for the last five years with this same air service. I guess I could relate to him in a way; he was a restless soul but had all the attributes of a competent pilot – and looked the part as well. He was maybe half a foot taller but reminded me of the duct tape guy, Red Green, in how he dressed in flannel, suspenders and that hat with the floppy brim but I didn't believe Red Green normally wore hip waders.

"Bob, what's the flight time to our destination anyway?" I asked.

"About forty to forty-five minutes almost due west once we are up and away," Bob answered.

"I guess that's why they call it Forty Minute Lake," Whitney mused.

"Maybe it takes forty minutes to walk around it," I suggested.

The Dehavilland Beaver on floats was a workhorse; it didn't even so much as groan when Bob reached top speed and lifted the aircraft off of the smooth water. Judging by the room and seats in the plane, we could've carried twice the load and passengers than the three of us and our gear, maybe even more.

Whitney had her face glued to the side window and was looking out of the plane as we ascended to an altitude of 2000 feet as indicated by the altimeter on the instrument panel. Seeing the picturesque countryside on such a clear day was a bonus for us both. Whitney had never witnessed the raw beauty of Alaska in this manner and the pleasure it brought to her was evident in the smile on her face.

The ground was covered in spruce trees that were dark green and what I believed to be tundra that was more brown and red than green. As far as the eye could see there were rivers, streams and many lakes dotting the landscape. I couldn't imagine any other wilder or more remote landscape anywhere. The vegetation and trees were thicker closer to water. The brown and red ground cover and low vegetation was prominent on the hills and areas farthest from water.

Bob would occasionally point downward and then steer to one side or the other and we would spot a moose or occasional bear on the ground or in one of the many ponds and lakes.

In about forty-five minutes we were on final approach to what looked like a puddle of water in front of the plane. As we descended and got closer to the puddle, it began resembling a lake of about forty acres in size. The dark water of the lake indicated to me it was deep. The lake itself was situated in the center of a group of hills that surrounded the lake on all sides and had huge spruce trees and willow bushes along the shore all around the water's edge.

The plane slowed and gracefully touched down on the flat and calm water of the lake and taxied toward the west edge where I could see a small floating dock on the water and a small cabin on the lake shore adjacent to the dock. This was the only sign of man on this lake and it was home for Whitney and me for the next few days. There was a flat bottom boat of about twelve feet in length tied to one side of the dock and Bob skillfully glided and maneuvered the plane to a stop close enough to the opposite side of the dock for him to stand on one of the floats and lasso a cleat on the dock with a small rope and pull the plane alongside the small pier and tie off.

"If the fishing is good, we'll be here for more than just a couple days," I said to Bob as we unloaded our gear.

"No problem Jake, I'll wait for your call but if I haven't heard from you in a couple of days I'll be back to pick you up as planned," Bob replied.

I'd been watching Whitney. She'd already wandered off and was at the cabin and quickly disappeared inside. I assumed to ensure it was okay before her only ride back to town had left her stranded. In just a couple minutes she exited the cabin and I could see she was all smiles.

"That's fine Bob, excellent flight by the way, thank you."

"My pleasure; you two have a great time and oh yeah, congratulations on your wedding," Bob added as he untied the plane from the dock and pushed away, climbed in and shut the door.

Within minutes I was standing on the dock alone, watching that beautiful plane glide across the water and gently take flight and disappear over the hills back in the direction of Dillingham.

As I was engrossed in watching the plane leaving, not paying any attention to what was behind me, Whitney quietly snuck up on my blind side and pushed me off of the dock and into the deep and frigid water. Laughing and running back toward the cabin, Whitney was obviously quite pleased with herself and feeling happy. The honeymoon had officially begun for the Rohn's!

Chapter 10

Blaine Alexander had no sooner dropped off Jake and Whitney at Shannon's Pond than his phone rang.

"Hello."

"Blaine, this is Lieutenant Rivers. There's been a report made of an overdue hiker up on the Agulowak River from the Chesterfield Lodge located there. I need you to come by the office and get the details and make the initial response. This may turn into a search and rescue and I would prefer to have you running things on location should it come to that."

"Sure thing lieutenant; I can be there in ten minutes."

Lieutenant Shane Rivers was the trooper commander for the Bristol Bay region and was stationed at the Dillingham post. Blaine knew him well and also knew he was a busy man. Lieutenant Rivers was leaving later in the morning for a scheduled visit to Dutch Harbor for an area wide meeting that, among other things, was covering domestic violence and alcohol related crimes occurring in the villages of that region.

"Hi Mary, is the lieutenant still here?" asked Blaine as he entered the trooper office.

Mary Peters, a short woman with black hair and brown eyes looked at Blaine over the top of her computer. Mary was an excellent and dependable worker but was known for her no-nonsense nature. She had worked as the clerk, evidence custodian and sometimes dispatcher for the troopers in Dillingham for more than fifteen years. She was born and raised in Dillingham and she knew every single person and family in the region.

"Don't try to be sweet to me Blaine Alexander; I'm still ticked off at you for that mess you made in the break room with your muddy boots the other day. Where does it say I'm your mother and I'm the one elected to clean up your mess?"

Blaine had dreaded this tongue lashing but knew he deserved it. "Okay Mary, I promise to make it up to you – really – but right now I have to see the lieutenant."

"I know Blaine; he's in his office. I've given him all the information on the initial report from the Chesterfield."

"Thanks," said Blaine as he scurried past Mary's desk and went into the lieutenant's office.

Behind the desk was Lieutenant Rivers. The troopers looked so sharp in their light blue shirts and dark blue pants with the gold stripe and red piping. Maybe he should've taken them up on one of the dozen or so requests he'd received to apply for the troopers and attend the academy in Sitka. Every lieutenant and sergeant that comes through this post has tried talking him into applying to do just that. His heart was here; he had no desire to leave the area and people he loved so much.

"Ready for the trip south, lieutenant?" Blaine asked.

"Yeah, but I have to fly three-hundred miles north to Anchorage in order to go south to Dutch Harbor," Rivers practically moaned.

"Tell me what we have and I'll get right on this call and get out of your way," said Blaine.

"Well," Rivers started. "Earlier this morning we received a call from the manager at the Chesterfield Lodge. It seems that one of their clients, a guest there for five days, left to do some hiking and fishing along the Agulowak River yesterday afternoon but failed to return to the lodge last night as anticipated. They thought this was unusual since he hadn't done this in the past and they didn't believe he was really prepared to stay out over-night."

"Anything about his health or demeanor that we should be concerned about?" inquired Blaine.

"Not really. His name is Ronald Spaulding and this is the second year in a row he's stayed at the lodge. He spent a week there last year and was set to do the same this year. He's fifty-three years old and reportedly is in fairly good health. He stays there alone and is generally quiet. By all reports he gets along fine with everyone and hasn't showed any sign of distress."

"What about his family?"

"I've contacted his wife in Washington State. She heard from him two days ago and everything was fine. She says he's above average in his outdoor skills and doesn't think he would get lost. She's standing by for any news that we have for her. Everyone at the lodge looked for Ronald last night and they're looking right now. Can you get a couple of guys together and get a hasty search going and then start a grid search? If Ronald got turned around or hurt he needs to be found today. Get some food, water and other supplies from the A.C. store on my state account. If my troopers aren't back here later today, call King Salmon and keep one of the troopers there briefed on your progress. Keep track of who is searching, and what areas are covered. I have a call in to Anchorage requesting a K-9 to assist if we don't have success right away," explained Rivers.

"Sure thing lieutenant. I'll take four or five of the locals with me; they know those woods well. That river is a wild and turbulent stretch of water between Lake Nerka and

Aleknagik Lake – it would be bad news for someone to fall into that."

"Thanks Blaine; we can get started on this and acquire more resources as time goes on."

"Lieutenant, did you know that Jake Rohn and his wife are in town, or were? I dropped them off a little while ago. They caught a charter that took them out to Forty Minute Lake where they have planned to stay a few days…it's their honeymoon."

"Yeah, Jake called me last week and told me. I forgot about it though. Things are so busy all the time out here that I can barely remember who I am."

"I'll get on this lieutenant and keep your guys in the loop," said Blaine as he headed to the door.

Chuck Jones viewed the text that had popped in on Baxter's phone sometime the previous night. Nice picture of the VPSO that Rohn had sent Baxter. So, that settles it: Baxter was definitely there as a lookout for Rohn.

'Stupid pricks! Do they think an amateur is after Rohn? I just might have to pay that asshole in Denver a visit for making this so damn difficult with his stupid bullshit bullet prank. Naturally, Rohn is gonna be more careful now. I now know he has at least told the VPSO what's going on, heaven

knows who else Rohn told. I can't go around killing every cop in this shitty little town. Maybe I should throw in the towel, but the fucking money is so damn good for this job.'

After witnessing the VPSO take Rohn to Shannon's Pond and leaving him and Whitney there, Jones had made a few calls to some air charters earlier that morning. Just by asking about the availability of charter planes he found one particular charter service that was taking a newlywed couple out to a remote lake and dropping them off for a few days. People were so willing to tell others their business if you just asked a few questions and then sit back and listen.

'Dammit,' thought Jones. *'Now Rohn and his lady have flown out of town for a couple of days and I don't see how I can do anything but wait. This place is too damn small to ask many questions. People will get suspicious. Maybe I should go up to Aleknagik Lake and do some fishing of my own. I hope no one discovers Baxter too soon. Sorry son-of-a-bitch...too bad I spotted him first! Crap, I'm hungry.'*

Jones was startled by the vibration of Glenn Baxter's phone that he had placed in his shirt pocket. The vibration was followed by the old T.V. show Hawaii 5-0's theme song. *'Go figure,'* thought Jones.

Jones looked at the front of the phone and saw that there was an incoming call but there was no number associated with it. '*I suppose I can speculate all day long who's calling this phone, it could be anyone.*' Jones shrugged and put the phone back into his shirt pocket, not giving it a second thought.

Chapter 11

I felt as if my arms were going to fall off. I believe I had rowed our boat all over that lake but the good news was that we caught so many rainbows that I lost count. I kept two fat specimens for our dinner later that evening. Even Whitney was catching fish.

The lake was as beautiful from our ground view as it was from the air. Spruce and willows crowded the banks all around. A sea of green surrounded the beautiful dark blue water of the lake. Grass and lilies were growing in the water along the shallow areas closer to the shore. We caught most of our fish near that vegetation.

"What kind of fish are these again?" Whitney asked for at least the fourth time.

"Rainbow trout," I answered patiently. I couldn't get frustrated with Whitney; she was so cute in her fishing hat, shorts and girly t-shirt. She was gaining a strong love of fishing and getting better with each cast and fish she landed which I removed from her hook each time.

"Tomorrow, I want to get across the lake to the outlet and hopefully we can find some pike," I announced between rowing strokes.

"What's a pike?" asked Whitney.

"You'll find out tomorrow. Let's head back to the cabin and get these fish on to cook; I'm starving."

I had to admit that I was worried about Glenn Baxter. I tried calling his phone earlier, utilizing the satellite phone I had brought with us but all I got was his voicemail. I left a message telling him I was just checking in, that we were staying at the remote cabin as planned and he would hear from me soon. We all have that little voice in our head that sometimes tries to get our attention or even point us in a different direction; mine was jumping up and down, screaming at me.

After returning to the dock, I stayed behind and quickly cleaned the two fish. Whitney went ahead of me and disappeared into the one room cabin. I knew that she was trying to impress me by making a fire in the wood stove in order for us to be able to cook our meal. I decided to take a few minutes to call Mark Dillon before I had to go save the day and start the fire for her.

After one ring Mark answered my call.

"Hi Mark."

"What's happening there Jake? Did Whitney leave you already?"

"You're a funny guy Mark; in fact she professes her love to me on an hourly basis. I satisfy her beyond imagination."

"So what's the real reason you called? I know it wasn't to try and convince me that you're superman in the sack. This phone costs the taxpayers a lot of money to use."

Mark was holding back a huge belly laugh, I could tell.

"You have me confused with Barry Simms; he's the guy that'll waste sat phone minutes calling 1-900 numbers."

With that comment, Mark couldn't hold it in any longer...he roared with laughter. I could hardly contain my laughter as well.

"Mark, have you heard from Glenn Baxter? I saw him last night at the airport when we got in but I haven't heard from him or seen him since then. I sent him a text message and have called his phone."

Mark had gained his composure quickly, this was business now. "No, I was actually waiting to hear from one of you. I'll try and reach him after we disconnect."

"The only person who knows about what is going on is the VPSO in Dillingham, Blaine Alexander. I introduced you two last summer when Blaine was attending some training in Anchorage and he had stopped by to see me."

"Yeah, I recall meeting him. Okay, I trust your judgment on this. We're really taking a chance keeping this quiet for now. Things best not go crazy," said Mark.

"You're telling me, crazy includes the possibility that I wind up pushing up daisies."

I could barely hear Mark's reply. "You...ly...est...call...er..."

Satellite phones aren't always reliable and it seemed that we were losing our connection.

"Mark, if you can hear me, I'm losing you. I'll call you back tomorrow," and with that I pushed the end button on the phone.

I grabbed up the freshly cleaned fish and started back toward the cabin. When I was about thirty feet away, I saw a jubilant Whitney come bounding from inside the cabin. She looked like the cat that had swallowed the canary.

"I did it and you doubted me."

I knew exactly what she meant; I could see the smoke coming from the tin smoke stack protruding from the roof. I was an investigator for heaven's sake. I couldn't resist messing with Whitney at least a little bit.

"Did what?" I said, acting clueless.

"You know, you said I could never do it."

"Catch a fish? I never said you couldn't catch a fish."

"No, you told me last night I could never do it all by myself."

"Honestly Whitney, I don't know what you mean, unless it's cleaning the fish and I already did that."

I thought I detected a bit of smoke coming from Whitney's ears. Okay, enough teasing her, she had lost her smile and was starting to get upset.

"You started the fire in the woodstove all by yourself; I was just messing with you."

"Jacob, you can be such a jerk at times."

I really loved this woman and now I felt bad that I'd spoiled her moment like I did. I spent the better part of an hour complimenting her for making such a wonderful fire. That's when I decided I was going to tell her what was going on. She had a right to know, hell; she was part of it just as much as anyone. Though I'd decided to come clean with Whitney, I thought it was best to wait until morning. We had one fantastic meal of these fresh rainbows to finish cooking and enjoy.

Chapter 12

Jenny Paul had seven of the most wonderful days off from work. Today was her first day back to her job at the Bay View B&B. She had enjoyed the time with her two kids and husband. They spent some time hiking, fishing and picking berries during the long days of summer and spending time with friends and family during the evenings. She also helped her mother prepare and smoke enough salmon to last the family throughout the winter. The rest of the time she played with and often read aloud to her young children. Her family was her life. After all, she had been raised by a mother whose life to this very day revolved around tending to her family – preparing Jenny to do the same.

She worked part time at the Bay View while she held down an almost full schedule of classes at the University of Alaska extension in Dillingham. Her goal was to earn a degree in education that would allow her to begin working locally as a teacher's aide in the preschool system in Dillingham and of course eventually become an actual teacher herself.

She never understood why the Bay View was still referred to as a bed and breakfast anyway. Since the rooms had all been updated with their meager kitchens, the only breakfast offered was muffins and coffee in the main office area. Not her worries; just get her work done and finish college.

This day she had a four hour schedule at work; her first task was to help the other part time employee clean the occupied rooms. Twelve of the twenty rooms currently had registered guests staying in them; if she cleaned six rooms and her co-worker did six rooms, they would be finished in just a couple of hours.

That was exactly how things worked out. At about an hour and a half into her routine, Jenny stopped in front of cabin number thirteen, the same cabin that was registered to Glenn Baxter. Jenny didn't get the note left behind at the front desk letting the cleaning crew know not to clean cabin thirteen until otherwise instructed. She was completely unaware of the grisly events that had occurred behind the locked door of the room she was about to enter.

As was her normal routine, Jenny knocked on the door and announced herself so that she did not walk in and surprise a guest in an awkward situation. "Housekeeping," she spoke in a loud and clear voice.

She heard no sounds from behind the door; no one answered. That was exactly what Jenny expected; after all, the occupants of these rooms were always gone by that time of day. She unlocked the door with her master key and stepped inside of the room after once again announcing herself. It was dark, so she turned on a table lamp.

The room appeared untouched. There was an open suitcase on the completely made bed. A shaving kit and towel were on a small table to one side of the room and some clothes on a chair and that was it.

"Sweet!" Jenny said aloud. "This is going to be quick."

Jenny went to work tidying up the small room and kitchen area. Her last chore was to clean up the bathroom and she would be done cleaning for the day. Inside the small bathroom she saw some water spots on the sink and the toilet seat was up. After completing a quick wipe down and replenishing the towels, Jenny was satisfied that the bathroom was clean, so she returned to the main room and was prepared to leave the cabin.

'Dammit,' she thought. 'I need to check the shower and wipe it down too if it had been used.'

Jenny re-entered the bathroom. The stand alone shower had a white plastic door across the front which was closed. She opened the shower door and let out a horrific shrieking scream and ran out of the bathroom and out the door of the cabin into the warm sunshine of the day. The entire time she was screaming at the top of her lungs as the image of a naked, and dead, Glenn Baxter seated on the floor of the shower was burned forever into her memory.

Chapter 13

Blaine Alexander made the fifty minute boat trip to the Chesterfield Lodge in deep thought. Aleknagik Lake was about twenty-five miles long and five miles across at its widest point. The lake was nestled in between peaks ranging from 800 to 1500 feet high. There was still some snow on the higher peaks above the tree line. The lake itself was lined with dark green spruce, willows and an occasional birch as well as a myriad of other species of low, thick brush. The water was as much as 380 feet deep and was mostly a constant 58 degrees Fahrenheit.

The lake was magnificent and was known for the red salmon spawning run that made its way up the Wood River from Bristol Bay and into the lake. The lake also was home to a massive population of arctic char that followed the smelt up the rivers, as well as some pike in the shallow and weed infested bays around the fringes of the lake. Rainbow trout could be found at the mouths of water inlets and rivers around the lake. The lodge was located along the Agulowak River, a world renowned rainbow trout fishing paradise.

The Chesterfield sat about two miles up the Agulowak River from Aleknagik Lake itself. As it was isolated, a boat was the only real method of reaching the lodge. A floatplane could get you close but then you would have to walk or take a boat the rest of the way.

Those unfamiliar with the Agulowak River were better off to leave navigation by boat to those who were not only skilled at operating a riverboat but intimately familiar with the river itself. With a fast current, boulders, jagged rocks and hidden shallows, this stretch of rainbow trout heaven that connected two major lakes could be a fatal trap for unsuspecting fisherman and adventurists who unwittingly braved the inconspicuous dangers of the Agulowak.

Blaine was familiar with the treacherous river but always felt a sense of relief once he arrived at the lodge. Once he parked and tied off his boat he made the short walk to the main lodge building.

Blaine knew the manager of the lodge fairly well and usually got to know the staff over the summer months. This year was different for some reason. He wasn't sure if he'd actually met any of the staff working at the lodge this year; this was his first trip to the Chesterfield Lodge all summer.

He hated this type of scenario; a lost fisherman or hiker in some of the harshest wilderness imaginable. It was more than twenty miles to the village of Aleknagik from the Agulowak River. That was the closest community. There were a few other lodges in addition to the Chesterfield in the area but unless Ronald Spaulding knew exactly where he was going, chances are he wouldn't find them.

Once he arrived at the main building he saw that the crew of volunteer searchers he had called upon had already arrived. There were six of them all together. They had grown up in this country and were eager and ready to begin their search.

Blaine immediately located and met with the lodge manager, Chase Rayburn.

Chase was a retired school teacher from Dillingham and was very familiar with what it took to manage a remote fishing lodge such as the Chesterfield. Some called him Clint because he was tall and thin and had gray hair and at first glance he actually resembled Clint Eastwood.

"Hi Chase, I wish we were going fishing or something else. Meetin' you under such circumstances isn't a good thing."

"I know what you mean. Let me fill you in on what we have going on. I met Spaulding last year about this time when he stayed here for a week. He likes to fish and to hike and that's what he's been doing on a daily basis since he arrived five days ago. He had two more days before he was scheduled to check out and return to Dillingham," Chase explained.

"Have you checked his room?" Blaine asked.

"Yeah, nothing extraordinary there; his things all seemed to be there but the fishing gear, hiking boots and daypack I normally saw him with are all gone," answered Chase.

"Who last saw Spaulding?"

"There are only five employees, and including Spaulding we have fourteen guests. He talked with one of the cooks about 2:00 p.m. yesterday. He stopped by the kitchen to get some snacks and water to take with him. Spaulding said he was going to do some fishing and hiking along the river but planned to be back to eat. Supper time was 7:00 in the evening just like every day. He had his gear with him but no one knows which way he went."

Blaine could sense that Chase was rather concerned. It wasn't normal for guests to wander off and get lost, or worse.

"Was Spaulding staying here at the lodge with anyone?" Blaine asked.

"No, he was alone."

"What have you told the staff and other guests?"

"I gathered all the staff and guests together earlier today. Everyone was briefed on the situation and collectively they were asked about what they may have seen or known about Spaulding but the best I could come up with was the cook who saw him before he took off fishing yesterday afternoon. I had the staff looking for Spaulding last night and earlier today with the help of some lodge guests."

"You've done well. I'm going to brief the search team and get them started by searching the river between the two lakes and the trails along the banks of the river and hope we find something to at least narrow our area of focus."

Blaine had stopped off at the State Parks office in Aleknagik and met with Cecil Peck, the ranger for the Wood-Tikchik State Park which included the area where we believed the missing fisherman was lost. Peck had been unaware of the overdue angler but was willing to travel to Dillingham and obtain the Cessna 172 aircraft available to him and begin flying over the vicinity hoping he could spot Spaulding.

Just after briefing the search teams and providing them their initial search areas, Blaine heard a familiar voice calling him over his handheld VHF radio. It was Cecil Peck, the park ranger/pilot.

"Go ahead for Blaine Alexander," Blaine spoke loud and clear into the handheld radio.

"Blaine, I'm just reaching the Agulowak River to the north of the lodge. Do you have additional information? I have one spotter on board, standing by for further instructions," boomed the voice of Peck over the radio.

Blaine explained that there was nothing more to add at the present time other than that the initial searching by the lodge employees and guests hadn't turned up anything that would help locate or even narrow down the search area for Spaulding. Blaine went on to elucidate that he had two, three man crews in boats searching the entire Agulowak where it was believed Spaulding went fishing and two additional three man crews, one on each side of the river, searching from Lake Nerka to Aleknagik Lake.

Blaine instructed Peck to concentrate his aerial search along the four mile long Agulowak River and the banks of Lake Nerka and Aleknagik Lake nearer the source and mouth of the river. Each team on the ground had a hand held VHF radio for communication with the aircraft, search base or other search teams if necessary.

Blaine felt he had the initial search response covered well enough. He went to Spaulding's room and checked it over with Chase Rayburn in tow. He didn't find a single clue that shed any light on where Spaulding had gone. Blaine also spoke with the remaining staff and guests at the lodge. Once again he came up empty with anything more that could help.

Blaine made his way to the main lodge where there was a satellite phone available. He called the trooper post in Dillingham but after speaking with Mary Peters and briefing her on where the search for Spaulding stood he still needed to call King Salmon and brief one of the troopers there since all the Dillingham post troopers were still unavailable.

After two rings a male voice came on the line, "This is Trooper Kramer, how may I help you?"

"Hey Donny, this is Blaine from Dillingham."

"Hi Blaine, I was expecting to hear from you. The lieutenant called me earlier and briefed me on what you have going over there."

"Okay, good; that saves time. I've checked things out here and there's nothing new to report. Everything seems to indicate that Ronald Spaulding went fishing as we were originally told and hasn't returned. We aren't certain exactly where or which direction he went other than somewhere along the Agulowak River."

"Good work Blaine. What do you have going as far as a search?"

"Ranger Peck is up in his aircraft with a spotter flying the river corridor and lake shores near the river. Two boats with searchers are checking the entire river and its banks. There are two additional search teams on foot, one on each side of the river scouring trails and looking for any sign of Spaulding."

"Sounds good Blaine. Have you talked with the lodge staff and guests?" asked Donny.

"Yeah, there are eighteen in all. Everyone has the same basic information except the cook and from him we learned that Spaulding left the lodge at about 2:00 p.m. yesterday to go fishing along the river. The cook was also able to tell us that Spaulding took meager supplies with him – about what you would expect someone to take with them on a day trip and that was the last time anyone saw Spaulding," explained Blaine.

"I've been looking at some information on search models to fit your scenario. Generally speaking, someone of Spaulding's age, fitness and experience level would stay close to water and with twenty hours passing since he left the lodge, he could have traveled seven to ten miles given Spaulding's average speed considering the terrain and brush in the search area," Donny added.

"What if he's sick or experienced some type of trauma? Could that change how he may react – especially if his level of adrenaline shot up?" Blaine asked.

"Absolutely. We just need a place to concentrate the search to begin with and expand as time goes by," Donny said.

"Do you want me to stay here then?"

"Yeah, that would be best for the time being. I'll arrange for someone to deliver food and water to Aleknagik if you can get there by boat in a couple of hours and pick up the supplies. Keep documenting the search area and the results. I believe we'll be able to get a K-9 to you by early in the morning – a handler and his dog are on their way to Anchorage from Fairbanks and should be in Dillingham later this afternoon and hopefully by then one of the Dillingham troopers will be able to get him out to the lodge; otherwise you'll need to pick him up yourself. Until then, call me every four to six hours for an update, or sooner if you find something significant."

"You got it Donny. I'll head back to Aleknagik in a while to pick up those supplies; I don't believe I brought enough out with me to last more than a day for all the volunteers who are helping."

After hanging up the phone, Blaine got the oddest feeling; of the countless search and rescues he's been a part of, this one seemed wrong somehow.

Chapter 14

A very timid and pale Chantra Bailey scurried out of the dispatch cubicle and down the hall to the chief's office and without knocking barged right in through the closed door. A startled Frank Perry looked up from his seat behind his work cluttered desk at his newest dispatcher. His first inclination was to chastise Bailey for barging in as she did but quickly realized that something had scared or at least surprised her and thought it best to find out what caused her to look and behave as she was.

"Chief!" Chantra swallowed hard but continued. "There's a dead body at the Bay View, the desk clerk called. One of the cleaning crew found it in cabin thirteen; they say it's a murder."

Frank Perry first began law enforcement when he was twenty-five years old. He worked for several small police departments on the east coast but was unable to find the right fit for him over a restless ten year career as a cop. He liked law enforcement but he wanted more than the normal patrol and investigative functions he was constantly asked to do – he wanted to connect with the people he was sworn to protect; he wanted to make a difference. He and his wife had moved to

Dillingham fifteen years earlier where he quickly landed a job with the Dillingham PD.

The work there was certainly different from what it had been back east earlier in his career. In this tiny fishing community in south central Alaska he found a home. There was such diversity during the busy spring and summer months with the influx of fishermen, cannery workers and other seasonal employees who flocked to the region and a much quieter and unique closeness to the area in the winter months. He took that time to really learn about the people and culture in the town he and his wife had elected to call home.

His efforts paid off. For the last four years he's been the top cop in Dillingham. He was hired as the Chief of Police after the long-standing chief, and his mentor, retired after nearly twenty years of running the PD.

"A dead body!" Chief Perry exclaimed as he came up out of his chair. "Okay, call EMS and have them respond with our patrol unit. I'm on my way," the chief gave firm directions to the unsettled Chantra Bailey as he donned his hat and strapped on his gun belt before heading outside to his vehicle.

It was a short drive to the Bay View B&B but when Chief Perry arrived his officer and an ambulance were already there. Officer Sharkey and a paramedic met the chief.

"Sharkey, what do we have?" the chief asked directly of his patrolman.

"Well chief," began the young cop. "In the bathroom of cabin thirteen is a deceased male. He's white and I would guess he's in his middle sixties. He has a single wound around his neck that looks as if it would be caused by strangulation. We just confirmed he was deceased and backed out of the room without disturbing anything."

"Do you recognize the victim?" asked the chief.

"No," said Sharkey.

"Nor do I," added the medic.

"Good job Sharkey, I want you to get over to the Bay View office and find out the name of the person who checked in to this room and everything about him that you can learn from the desk staff," directed Chief Perry.

Chief Perry entered cabin thirteen and noted everything about the scene before him. The room was relatively small with a queen sized bed, end table and dresser. There was a flat screen TV on the dresser. A small round table was off to the side and there was a cabinet with a microwave adjacent to a small sized refrigerator. There was no sign of forced entry or struggle within the room.

There was an open suitcase on the bed and a shaving kit on the table along with a towel. A pair of shoes was under the table and a pair of trousers, shirt and light jacket were all neatly hung on a chair that was pushed up to the table. Other than the few personal items, Chief Perry didn't see anything else in the room. In fact the room had the appearance of someone being there for only a very brief period and not having time to give the space that lived in look.

The door to the bathroom was just beyond the small table where the shaving kit sat. Upon entering, Chief Perry noted that the bathroom itself was neat and clean, with the exception of a dead man seated on the floor of the shower.

The scene in the bathroom was just as Officer Sharkey had described it. On the floor of the shower sat an older man who looked to have been strangled. There were distinct ligature marks around his neck as well as the usual petechial hemorrhaging around his eyes and in the whites of his eyes that's generally present when a person is killed in such a manner.

Chief Perry returned to the main room and searched through the pockets of the clothes draped over the chair and found a wallet in one of the back pants pockets. Though he looked about the room for a cell phone of the victim, he wasn't able to locate one. He retrieved the wallet and exited the cabin and dialed the PD on his own cell phone.

The photo on the driver's license he found in the wallet matched the victim.

Chantra Bailey answered the phone.

"Chantra, I need you to run an Alaska driver's license of our victim. It has the name Glenn Baxter with an Anchorage address."

"Chief, you said Glenn Baxter?" Chantra asked almost incredulously.

"Yeah, why?"

"Not five minutes ago a gentleman called here, asking for you but I told him you were out on a call. He said his name was Jacob Rohn. It sounded as if he was on a ship to shore phone or a satellite phone. He asked if Glenn Baxter had come to the PD but he didn't say why. He hung up or the connection was ended abruptly and I didn't have any information on how to call him back."

"Jake Rohn; he's an investigator from Anchorage. He was asking about Glenn Baxter?" Chief Perry asked.

"Yes chief he was, but I don't know why and we were disconnected before I could get any additional information. I found a Glenn Baxter in the computer, born in 1947 with an Anchorage address. He doesn't have any case involvement or criminal history."

"Okay Chantra, run Baxter through NCIC and all other record locators you can find and print them for me. If Rohn calls back, find out how to reach him and call me at once. Look in the rolodex on my desk, find and text me the number for Mark Dillon. You're doing a great job handling things there."

As Chief Perry ended the call to Chantra, Officer Sharkey joined him in front of cabin thirteen.

Before Officer Sharkey was able to speak, Chief Perry began. "So the guy in number thirteen checked in yesterday, his name is John Smith and he paid cash. Other than that they couldn't give you much more information?"

Officer Sharkey looked confused. "Well actually his name is Mark Smith, but yeah, he paid several days in advance with cash and he did check-in yesterday but no one has seen him since. He called the office not long after arriving and asked not to be disturbed but the cleaning lady who found him didn't get the message."

"Sharkey, something big is going on here and we weren't invited to the party. I need you to stay here and keep this crime scene secure and get information on every guest registered here as well as the staff working here. I'll send a second officer to assist you and then I have some calls to make. I want you both to stay together and keep your eyes peeled to any hint of danger."

"Got it chief!" Sharkey confidently reassured Chief Perry.

Chapter 15

I just couldn't wait until morning to tell Whitney; the secrecy was making me nuts. Telling her everything up until now was easy; the hard part was dealing with the silent treatment and horrible stares she was giving me.

"Whitney, I was wrong for keeping this from you but I thought I was protecting you and at the same time not spoiling your happiness. I made a choice and that choice wasn't the right thing to do; I see that now and I'm truly sorry."

For the longest time I thought I had screwed up so bad that there was no way Whitney was going to forgive me.

"I also think it's best we cut our trip short and get back to Dillingham and then to Anchorage. At least then we can work on this with the help of Mark Dillon and the rest of the unit. We can't live in fear Whitney; this is something I need to face. We can decide together the best and safest steps for us both."

Finally, after what seemed like hours, Whitney spoke up. "Jacob, I understand you were only trying to protect me, to protect us both. You were wrong for not telling me sooner but I respect your decision. But I'm happy you told me now."

Whitney came to me and we embraced. I was really agonizing over this entire situation but the one thing I couldn't forgive myself for was not knowing or believing that Whitney was strong enough to face this with me. I should've known better. I was amazed at her composure. She could teach me some skills in how to remain calm.

"I contacted the air taxi and with some begging I was able to talk them into getting to us first thing in the morning. I expect that the plane should arrive by about 8:00 or 8:30 a.m.," I explained to Whitney.

I was pretty worried on the inside since I couldn't reach Baxter or Blaine by phone. The only solace I had at the moment was that I had come clean with Whitney and it was good to have her support.

It was getting late in the day when Blaine Alexander finally made it to the boat launch in Aleknagik. He met with the driver that Trooper Kramer was able to enlist to deliver the supplies from Dillingham. They would be needed by the searchers that were still actively searching for Ronald Spaulding who'd been missing for well over a day now.

The only real progress made was the discovery of Spaulding's daypack along a trail adjacent to a favorite fishing spot on the river perhaps a mile from the lodge where

Spaulding had been staying. The pack was leaning up against a tree and looked as if it was placed there, rather than dropped or otherwise accidentally separated from Spaulding.

The pack contained water, maps, matches, food and extra clothes and a bit of fishing tackle. The daypack was identified by staff and guests of the lodge as belonging to Spaulding. The location and how the pack was discovered made the entire situation seem even stranger but Blaine thought he had a last known position for Spaulding and they could concentrate the search efforts from there.

Finding the pack created more questions than answers. There were no animal tracks or signs of anything that would explain the disappearance of Spaulding. It was as though the earth opened up and swallowed him. The belief was that he fell into or somehow wound up in the swift current of the Agulowak River. If that was indeed what happened, he wouldn't be the first that met their demise in that manner.

It had been a few hours since he spoke to Trooper Kramer, so Blaine took the opportunity to call him while he had cell phone service in Aleknagik.

When Trooper Kramer answered, Blaine cut to the chase. "Hello Donny, this is Blaine. I'm in Aleknagik picking up those supplies. The search teams have been at it for hours and since my last contact with you, one of the ground teams found Spaulding's daypack which has been positively identified."

"That's good news; any sign of Spaulding then?" asked Donny.

"No, but I've concentrated the search efforts from that location. But nothing more has been discovered. Everyone thinks he drowned," Blaine said in a sorrowful tone.

"Odd, déjà vu," Donny thought out loud. "We had a search and rescue north of King Salmon a while ago - near Igiugig where a fisherman was lost. They found his hat near the river and that was it. It's believed he drowned too."

"Alright Donny, I'll keep you informed of any progress. Cecil Peck was only able to give us four hours of flying time today but he came up empty. He will be back at it in the morning'. If there's any sign of Spaulding in the water or shoreline, he'll find it."

"Oh, Blaine, before I forget – I know you and Jacob Rohn are friends. Did you know he was in Dillingham?" asked Donny.

"Yeah, he and his new bride stayed with us yesterday but they are off fishing now. Why do you ask?" Blaine cautiously inquired.

"There's some big hoodoo going on in Dillingham with a guy named Glenn Baxter being killed and the police chief there is pissed because he thinks Rohn and this Baxter had something going and they didn't let him know about it. Just wondering if you heard anything about that since you were friends with Rohn."

Glenn Baxter! Blaine knew some but not all of what was going on. He felt he had better get to Dillingham and speak with Chief Perry. Rohn and Whitney both could be in grave danger.

"Donny, things are pretty well lined out with the search crews. I'm gonna have someone get these supplies up to the lodge. I think I should go see Chief Perry. I'll be able to meet that K-9 handler sooner and get him out to the search area quicker that way."

"Okay Blaine that seems reasonable. Keep me informed on any progress with the search," and Trooper Kramer disconnected the call.

Chapter 16

"I could give a rat's ass less! I should have been notified of the potential threat in my town, Dillon!" A red faced Frank Perry screamed into the speaker of his desk phone.

On the receiving end of that call was Mark Dillon.

"I haven't been able to reach Rohn. The last time I spoke to him the satellite phone Rohn was using lost its connection or something. Shit, he's on the edge of the world it seems like!" Boomed the exasperated voice of Mark Dillon from the speaker.

Frank Perry was clearly at his wit's end. He has what turned out to be an ex-fed dead at one of the most popular B&B's in town. The local trooper lieutenant and his troopers are out of the area. He called Mark Dillon only to learn that Jacob Rohn was honeymooning or some such nonsense while he was being targeted by some unknown hit man possibly hired by some other unknown assclown in Denver. Who could make up such ridiculous horseshit?

Perry tried to settle down some. All he had to do now was to secure the scene and wait for crime scene specialists from Anchorage. At first he was thinking this was some kind of drug investigation or something gone wildly wrong. The scene of Baxter's murder was screaming that it was a professional job. But no, now he has some maniacal hit man running loose in town apparently turning over every rock in his search for Rohn.

"Look chief, we screwed up by not telling you ahead of time. Honestly, I doubt things would've changed much but now we can't be Monday morning quarterbacking our play. I know Rohn confided in VPSO Blaine Alexander but he's up at the Chesterfield Lodge running a search and rescue operation for a missing fisherman. Rohn's with his bride and they're staying at a remote cabin but Blaine has the details of where they are."

Frank Perry was seated now and most of the red had drained from his face. "What do you suggest we do now?"

At that moment there was a solid knock on the chief's door.

"Who is it?" asked Chief Perry.

"VPSO Alexander," was the response from behind the closed door.

"Blaine, get in here!" growled the chief.

Blaine Alexander entered the office and closed the door behind him. This was becoming one of the longest days in recent memory for him. He took a seat in front of the chief's desk.

"Blaine, I'm on speaker phone with Mark Dillon, Rohn's supervisor. Have you met?" inquired Chief Perry.

"Sure we have," was the quick response from the speaker phone. "Hi Blaine, we met last year in Anchorage," said Mark Dillon.

"I remember," responded Blaine. "I heard that Glenn Baxter was found dead. Are Jake and Whitney okay?"

Chief Perry spoke up. "That's what we're trying to figure out right now. I didn't even know Rohn was in town and have no idea where he is. Mark knows they're at a remote cabin. We were hoping you could fill us in Blaine."

Blaine felt comfortable talking with Mark and the chief. "They're at Forty Minute Lake. While driving over I called the air charter that took them earlier this morning. Rohn has already called them and they'll be going out first thing tomorrow to bring them back here ahead of their original plans."

Mark chimed in. "When I spoke with Rohn earlier today he was concerned that he couldn't reach Baxter; perhaps his concern has prompted their early return. Rohn was using a sat phone but the connection was awful and I've been unable to reach him since."

"I haven't spoken to Rohn since leaving them at Shannon's pond this morning, but he did leave me a voicemail telling me he was checking in," added Blaine.

"Chief, is there any chance one of your officers may have noticed someone who was acting strange or drawing attention to themselves?" Mark Dillon asked.

"I've called in all our available patrols. I have six extra guys working in plain clothes; there are only ten of us anyway. We're doing what we can to turn up something but trying to keep a lid on this at the same time. I've no doubt that word of the death has spread but the details have been kept quiet. We get a hundred or more new faces in town daily. The turnover of the cannery workers and the hunting and fishing bring in a lot of newcomers every day," explained the chief.

"I like what you're doing chief. I suggest that we continue with your current plan and when we get Rohn back to Anchorage, I believe your threat will not be far behind him," said Mark.

"God, I certainly hope so," said the weary chief.

Blaine stood and shook hands with Chief Perry. "Sounds like a plan guys. I have to get some things together and work on getting back up to the lodge with that Trooper K-9 and handler that should arrive in town later. I'll keep my eyes peeled but I have to concentrate on that search and rescue at the moment."

Both Mark Dillon and Chief Perry wished Blaine success with the search as he left the PD. As he got into his vehicle and drove away from the PD, he couldn't shake a bizarre feeling that he was unable to pinpoint, that he was being watched.

Chuck Jones was busy blending in with the other anglers along the shore of Aleknagik Lake. He'd been watching activity at the boat ramp. There was some talk of a missing fisherman at one of the lodges. He figured that would keep the local cops busy trying to find the schmuck who got himself lost or eaten by a friggin' bear.

He was getting pretty good at this fishing thing. He'd caught and released maybe six fish while making small talk with other anglers that came and went as the day dragged on.

He was all legal, with an out of state fishing license and a copy of the fishing regs. A person needed a college degree to interpret the fishing regulations in Alaska. Holy crap! Treble hook, single hook, gap, bag limit, species, bait, artificial lure, night time, day time, fish length, where to legally hook a fish and not to mention spawning times, tides, closure periods and drainages.

It was a way to pass the time. He learned that Rohn was going to be gone for a few days so what the hell, enjoy this paradise they call Alaska!

Chapter 17

I woke up to a calm and beautiful morning. The water on the lake was like a mirror. I spent a good forty-five minutes sitting alone near the dock. After she woke and splashed water on her face to wash away the sleep from her eyes, Whitney joined me and together we enjoyed the morning unfolding in front of us and the wonderful sounds that came with it.

"How'd ya sleep?" I asked as Whitney settled in next to me.

"It's so quiet and peaceful out here. I'm sorry we're leaving earlier than planned," Whitney yawned and put her head on my shoulder.

We watched the morning come alive with waterfowl on the lake and squirrels and birds in the trees lining the shore. A beaver skillfully and quietly swam along one shore with branches in tow that he ripped or chewed from low brush. These were most likely for his home he was building or repairing somewhere close by even if we couldn't readily see it. A bull moose stood knee deep in the lake near the shore across from the dock with his head underwater much of the time in order to reach the plant growth in the shallows there. Occasionally the moose would raise his head and water would run off his massive rack as he stood proud while chewing the waterlogged vegetation.

"Our ride will be here soon; we should get our gear together so that we're ready when it does get here," I said as I rose and extended my hands to help Whitney to her feet.

"You're always the practical one Jacob," Whitney said with a smile.

We spent the next twenty minutes or so gathering and packing our gear. As I reached the dock with the last bag I could see our plane descending towards the lake from over the hills but I couldn't hear it. As the plane got closer I could definitely hear the engine power up as the pilot lowered the flaps and gently settled the stunning plane down onto the smooth surface of the lake. It was the same plane we arrived in the day before and I could only imagine Bob Johnson was the skillful pilot bringing the massive plane in for such a picture perfect landing.

In just a few minutes our air taxi was alongside the dock and I was helping Bob load our gear back into the plane.

"Nice landing Bob," I said when Bob first hopped out of the cockpit.

"Thanks Jake. Pilots have a saying that all landings you're able to walk away from are good," Bob said with a smile.

I could see the logic in that line of thinking. "I like your skills Bob; thanks for making it out here on such short notice. Shit happens and we just have to get back to civilization."

Whitney had joined us at the dock and she was both eager and hesitant to get back into the plane. I think she really liked our time at the cabin and wished we could stay but knew the reality of the situation and that it was best we leave.

As Bob stowed our last piece of gear he stopped and turned toward the two of us. "Speaking of shit happens, I think there was a shooting in town and someone was killed."

Okay, out went all the sentiment and glamour of the morning and of the beautiful landing of the plane on the lake. All the birds stopped singing. Whitney's smile turned into a scowl. I could feel the tightness in my throat cutting off not only my oxygen but my ability to speak.

"A shooting!" I said out loud once but silently under my breath at least two dozen times.

So many thoughts went through my head. It was an avalanche of feelings picking up speed and mass at it roared through my thought process. I was imagining the worst possible scenarios, all of which ended badly. I had to keep calm and restrain my fear – what else could have happened? I was afraid Glenn Baxter had been involved in a shooting while trying to protect me and Whitney; maybe he got the drop on the bastard sent to kill me.

"Well, I'm not sure what happened, but some guy died for certain. I heard so many different things I'm not positive what happened but I sort of liked the shooting story," Bob explained as he climbed into the cockpit.

As quickly as my fears escalated, they subsided somewhat. For all I knew someone had just fallen over dead. I know Bob was just making conversation but he couldn't have had any notion that his news would've had such a profound effect on me.

Almost an hour later we were landing at Shannon's pond. I could see a DPD patrol car parked near the air taxi's building. No sooner had Whitney and I climbed out of the plane and onto the dock than there was a young officer greeting us and then whisking us away.

"But how'd you know when we would arrive?" I asked the young officer.

"I don't know sir, the chief told me to meet your plane and take you to his office and that's exactly what I'm doing," replied the young patrolman.

Whitney was losing the color in her face again. I knew there was no reason to quiz this young man any longer. He wouldn't give up any information anyway; we would see Chief Perry soon enough and hopefully get a complete explanation.

I removed my cell phone from my pocket and turned it on. In less than a minute the phone powered up and I could see I had missed calls from Mark Dillon, Blaine Alexander and a couple from an unknown number. There were two voice messages but by then we arrived at the PD, so I didn't have time to check them.

We were escorted into a small sitting area and before I could be seated I was approached by Chief Perry who shook my hand and invited me to his office. Whitney said she would wait there while the chief and I spoke privately.

After the chief showed me to his office and I sat down he started. "Glenn Baxter was found dead yesterday in his room at the Bay View B&B."

I'd almost prepared myself for the news. Although I hoped the death Bob had mentioned was something completely unrelated, my cop sense kept telling me otherwise and had prayed I was wrong.

Chief Perry continued. "Rohn, I was mad as hell with you over this business but I've had time to calm down since speaking to Mark Dillon. He filled me in on what this was about and I can't say I agree with what your plan was, but I can't say I would've done anything differently either. There was no real evidence of any danger anyway. However, if I was potentially leading a professional killer to a town I would've notified the chief of police of the jurisdiction of the possible danger."

I felt as though I was getting a lecture from my dad, and just like my dad's lectures, I deserved this one too.

"Chief, I was wrong when I failed to inform you about what was going on but at this point we should concentrate on what happened to Glenn and decide what we're going to do now. Can you tell me what you found? Our pilot seemed to think someone had been shot."

"You're right Jake. Second guessing your decision to keep the threat under wraps won't change what happened; we need to move forward. There are two crime scene techs at the scene as we speak. I can tell you that Baxter wasn't shot; that's just rumor. He was strangled with a garrote of some sort. We know that Baxter checked in at the B&B two days ago. Not long after checking Baxter in; the desk clerk got a call asking them not to bother Baxter or his room because of the odd hours he'd be keeping. It seems to me that whoever killed Baxter got the drop on him fairly soon after he got to his room. The killer was obviously quite skilled; judging by the way he completed his task while remaining undetected and did an excellent job at hiding his work. The murder would have stayed undiscovered for a lot longer if one of the B&B staff hadn't entered the cabin to clean it not knowing that Baxter, or someone posing as Baxter, had called and made the request not to be disturbed."

"You're describing a professional hit," I said.

"That's exactly how I see it. That means you were most likely correct in the assumption that someone has put a contract out on you. The person after you is very accomplished at what they do. It's my understanding from Mark Dillon that Baxter was experienced in this type of operation. The question is how in the hell did the killer spot him anyway? We know that Baxter had used a DOT pickup to get to the B&B but we found it at the airport where it had been left for him. It's been towed to our garage for the crime techs to go over as well."

An avalanche of questions, fear and doubt plowed its way through my mind. All rational thoughts and self-confidence were buried by the onslaught of uncertainty. I felt completely responsible for Baxter's death as well as putting every person in Dillingham at risk – which included Whitney! I felt sick.

The chief was a wise man. He let me digest all this information and allowed time for my thought process to begin to click before he quizzed me. This man knew how to conduct an investigation and how to get information.

"Jake, one odd thing is we've been unable to locate a cell phone in Baxter's room or belongings. I can't imagine that he didn't carry one. His gun and credentials are also missing."

"He did carry a cell. It was a flip phone, I remember him answering it the day I met him in Anchorage and I was thinking who in the hell carries a flip phone these days. I remember the ring tone – the old Hawaii 5-0 theme song."

"We've been unable to find the phone. Maybe he'd lost it; maybe the killer took it along with his gun and badge. That's what we have to assume. Who knows what information the killer could acquire from that phone?"

"Oh shit! Chief – I sent Baxter a text with information and a photo of VPSO Blaine Alexander."

Chapter 18

VPSO Blaine Alexander slept quite poorly. Not only was he restless over what had happened to Glenn Baxter, he was also concerned for Jake and Whitney and their safety. He knew the two of them were returning to Dillingham this morning. Of course the search and rescue for Ronald Spaulding was coming up empty as well. The search for Spaulding had to be his main focus at the moment.

It wasn't only the stress of everything going on; Rufus woke him a couple of times during the night – barking his damn head off. That dog is certainly protective of their home but he's been known to chase off rabbits, fox and stray dogs with the same protective bark. Blaine had checked outside twice but there was nothing to be seen. He attributed his uneasiness and his being so jumpy to the recent goings-on.

He met Trooper Jarvis and his K-9, Spark, after they arrived to town the previous evening. The plan was to take the K-9 unit up to the last known point of Spaulding and hope that Spark may be able to track him. He and Trooper Jarvis had planned to be on the road by 5:00 a.m.

Blaine had called Trooper Kramer in King Salmon the prior evening and filled him in on the progress of the search for Spaulding; or the lack of progress to be more accurate. There had been no news from the search teams but plans had been made for two aircraft to continue the search the following morning; an additional fifteen to twenty volunteers would be available as well.

Blaine thought about his search and rescue training and hearing about similar searches in the lower forty-eight states. In those instances there would be literally hundreds of volunteers, several aircraft, a group of K-9 units and resources more readily available. In remote Alaska, those types of resources were slow in arriving. They had to utilize what was available and not worry about what they didn't have.

It was fifteen minutes before 5:00 a.m. when Blaine pulled up to the trooper bunkhouse and picked up Trooper Jarvis and Spark.

"Are you guys ready for this?" asked Blaine.

"We were born ready!" replied Trooper Jarvis.

Blaine liked to hear that. "The plan is to get you and Spark up to the search area. We can show you where the daypack of

Spaulding's had been found. Is that where you would like to start?"

"Absolutely! This is my first time in the Dillingham region. What's the search area like?"

"We're going to the Chesterfield Lodge which is located on the Agulowak River about twenty miles from Aleknagik. We can drive to Aleknagik but we have to take a boat the rest of the way via Aleknagik Lake and then up the river a short way. The terrain there is wooded with thick brush, obviously remote and unpopulated but it's mostly flat near the river and lake but completely surrounded by hills," answered Blaine.

"Quite like most of rural Alaska; okay I get the picture," said Trooper Jarvis. "We're raring to go!"

Blaine and Trooper Jarvis made the remainder of the trip in relative silence. Each was thinking hard about the task they had in front of them. Neither said it out loud but both were hoping for a quick and positive end to this search. Occasionally there was some small talk between the men but overall there was more thinking than talking.

It was a couple of hours before Blaine and the K-9 unit of Trooper Jarvis and Spark made it to the Chesterfield Lodge. Blaine received an update from the search teams. There was nothing positive to report other than the continued efforts of the searchers to find Spaulding in the dense woods. The search areas had been expanded as the search teams grew in numbers as more volunteers made it to the area. Spaulding had been missing for two nights now and he was certainly without any sort of supplies other than what may have been in his pockets.

Trooper Jarvis and Spark were taken to the spot where the daypack was found. The hopes were that they could find a trail or something that may lead to the area Spaulding had traveled to or outright find him. It would be hours before anything would be known from the efforts of the K-9 unit. Blaine remained at the lodge and assigned search areas to the new volunteers and continued making notations of the search effort in addition to gathering all information from the search teams that were returning to get new instructions and replenish their supplies.

The mood among the searchers, lodge employees and guests had become quite somber since Blaine had left. More than forty-eight hours had passed with no sign of Spaulding wasn't a good omen and everyone knew it.

It had been about four hours since the K-9 unit had left the Chesterfield to begin their search for Spaulding when one of the searchers came roaring back to the lodge on a four wheeler. The young man driving the ATV burst into the office where Blaine and Chase Rayburn were busy marking maps and making notes on information pertaining to the search.

"VPSO Alexander, Trooper Jarvis sent me back for you. He found something he wants you and Mr. Rayburn to see right away," said the winded messenger.

"We'll follow you," said Blaine as he grabbed for his hat and headed out the door with Chase Rayburn on his heels.

It took about ten minutes for Blaine and Chase to reach Trooper Jarvis. They doubled up on one four wheeler and followed the search volunteer who had come to get them at the lodge. The ride was wild but their hearts were racing with adrenaline at the prospects of finding Spaulding.

After stopping and dismounting the ATV, Blaine and Chase were met by Trooper Jarvis and Spark.

"Okay guys, bad news and not so bad news I guess," started Trooper Jarvis. "Up the river about a quarter mile next to where the daypack was found, Spark trailed Spaulding to the river's edge and that was it. I worked Spark in a circle hoping to find Spaulding's trail but all I found was his back trail that Spark and I followed to the lodge."

Blaine Alexander shifted back and forth wanting to interrupt but waited and listened to

Trooper Jarvis, not knowing where this was leading.

Trooper Jarvis continued. "I had Spark work the trail as close to the river's edge as possible from the lodge toward the mouth of the Agulowak River where it enters Aleknagik Lake. Right down close to the river from where we are now, Spark located a fly rod and small fishing net. I want Chase and some of the lodge guests to look at this rod and net but I have to tell you I'm pretty certain they both belong to Spaulding."

Chase had been listening but spoke up. "How can you be sure it's Spaulding's?"

Trooper Jarvis held up a fly rod and pointed to the base of the fiberglass pole. "Right there it has 'R. Spaulding' written on it."

"I don't get it; did Spark pick up a trail of Spaulding then?" Blaine asked.

"That's just it; these were in brush right next to the river but there wasn't any scent trail leading to them or even near them – they either fell from the sky or someone threw them onto the bank as they were floating by on the river," explained Trooper Jarvis. "The damndest thing I've ever seen while searching for a lost person."

Blaine spoke up. "Let's get these back to the lodge and ensure that they can be positively identified as Spaulding's. I'll also get to work on adjusting our search which seems to be taking us farther away from the lodge."

"I'll keep working Spark along this trail toward the lake and next to the river bank in hopes of finding any additional sign of Spaulding," said Trooper Jarvis.

While heading back towards the lodge, Blaine Alexander had that feeling again. This was the fourth time in two days. Something was entirely wrong about this search and rescue.

Chapter 19

"Right here, someone stood for at least twenty or thirty minutes," I said pointing to the ground next to a huge spruce tree.

Chief Perry walked over to where I stood, stopped and looked down to where I was pointing.

"See the footprints that are jumbled together where the soft ground was flattened out? Two cigarette butts alongside the footprints. A clear view of Blaine's home about fifty yards away," I added.

"Jake, I think you're right. Someone was watching Blaine's house."

"At least checking it out from a distance, maybe looking for me," I said.

The chief and I thought it best to check on VPSO Blaine Alexander's home after we realized that Baxter's missing cell phone contained information intended for Baxter about the VPSO. If someone got their hands on that information, that may put the Alexander's in danger if it was believed I was there or they may know where I was.

We rushed right over to the house to find Blaine's wife, Diane, busy with her daily routine. I was done with not being straight forward with people, especially with those that might be in danger. The chief and I sat down with Diane and told her exactly why we were there.

"I'm really happy the two of you came over and are telling me this now but Blaine left early this morning to get back to that search and rescue up at the Chesterfield Lodge," explained Diane.

"Yeah Diane, we know about the search and Blaine's roll there but we had to be sure you and your family were safe," I said.

"Blaine couldn't sleep anyway, with everything going on and Rufus barking half the night, and so he left earlier than planned," Diane added.

"Was something going on or was someone outside?" I asked.

"No, Blaine checked but couldn't see anything. Rufus will bark at animals that get too close to the house," Diane answered.

That certainly clenched the deal in my mind; someone was watching their home. It gave me that sickening feeling again, all of this because of me.

"Diane, I think it would be best if you could stay somewhere else for the time being. Just to be on the safe side. It would make matters worse for you or some of your family to get caught up in this just because someone was after me," I explained.

Diane seemed to come to the same conclusion rather quickly.

"Okay, we'll go stay with my mom and brother. They'll be glad to have us there," agreed Diane.

"Rufus too?" I asked.

"Of course, that big knucklehead is pretty handy to have around," said Diane as she patted that beast of a dog on top of the head.

We waited for Diane to call her mom and then get some things together. The chief and I followed Diane to her mom's house and once we were confident she was safely inside, we drove back to the PD.

"Chief I was just thinking, since we believe Baxter's killer took his cell phone, maybe we can use it against him and track it some way," I suggested.

The chief looked at me across his desk. "We don't have the luxury of that technology here. The best we can do is submit the number to the cell provider and in a few weeks get a printout of what cell towers the phone activated in the area when calls were made or received on the phone."

"Okay, how about the crime scene guys? Let's go see if they have anything helpful to report," I suggested.

"Let me call them and find out if they're finished at the B&B," said Chief Perry as he reached for his phone.

After a brief conversation, Chief Perry hung up his phone. "They're on their way back here now but it didn't seem as if they had anything really promising to report anyway."

I'd been so busy I hadn't taken time to call my boss, Mark Dillon. I took advantage of a little time that we had before the crime scene investigators arrived at the PD and called him.

"Hi Mark, how are things there?"

"Well, you know that diet I was considering? Not necessary any longer; I just lost about twenty pounds of ass from the chewin' that Julie Dancer just gave me. It seems that my idea to keep this all quiet wasn't very popular at all – it's not that we would've done anything differently in my opinion. Baxter knew the danger; we all did. I guess I should've insisted you stay here! Hell Jake, we didn't even know if there was a real threat! But that doesn't help anything. I wish there was something I could do to make this easier."

I didn't think anyone could have felt shittier over this than I did but I think Mark was coming pretty close.

"Mark, there's a flight leaving here for Anchorage in three or four hours. Whitney doesn't know yet but she'll be on it. Will you meet her and see to it that she's safe?"

"You got it Jake. What news do you have for me?"

I filled Mark in on everything right up until the point I called him. He agreed on the steps we were taking and wanted me to keep him informed.

"Thanks Mark for taking care of Whitney."

"No worries. You call me with any news. I think it would be best if you got on the plane with Whitney."

"Mark, there are only a fraction of the people here than in Anchorage. Don't you think it's a good idea that we give it a day or two in hopes this guy shows himself or tips his hand? It'll be much easier to spot him out here – and hopefully put an end to this madness."

"Okay Jake, two days; if nothing turns up you get your ass back here. For now, I have everyone's cooperation on this. I think that's about as long as I can hold off the wolves before they have us all for lunch."

"You got it. I'll keep you informed."

After ending my call with Mark Dillon I wandered back into the chief's office. I recognized the crime lab techs; one was Jeff Fleener who I knew to be very competent at crime scene investigation and had worked with several times over the last few years. The other was Carlos but I had seen him only once or twice and thought he was rather new.

"Sit down Jake. These two were just starting to give me a run down about what they uncovered at the crime scene," invited Chief Perry.

"Hi Jake," started Jeff Fleener as he waved his right hand as part of his greeting. "I was just filling in the chief on what we found in our investigation so far."

"Good to see you two out here so fast," I said. "Not the most ideal of circumstances, but it almost always means someone's dead when I run into you guys."

Jeff continued his verbal report. "We collected some latent fingerprints as well as a few fibers and hairs at the scene. We realize that the room is used by so many different people; our hopes are not sky high in identifying the killer from prints. The cause of death most certainly seems to be from strangulation but won't be verified until an autopsy is completed. There were no other injuries noted on Baxter's body. It appears certain that Baxter was killed near the bed and dragged into the shower – he had carpet fibers on his heels. There'd been no forced entry into the room but there were some scratches on the lock and on the door facing that we could possibly match to a long, thin bladed knife or other such tool. The strangulation weapon was most likely brought by the killer and then taken away as we were unsuccessful at locating any mechanism in the room that could have been used."

"Did you find a cell phone?" asked the chief.

"No phone was found at the scene," answered Jeff.

"Has Baxter's body been taken care of?" I asked.

"Currently his body is being stored at Kanakanak Hospital pending transport to Anchorage," said Jeff. "The chief tells me there may be another scene that we need to look at."

"Yeah there is; the chief can show you. We think there's a chance that the killer may have staked out the VPSO's house for a while and may have left some evidence behind," I explained.

"Let's get to it then," said Jeff as he stood and motioned for Carlos to follow.

"Chief, can you get these guys to Blaine's place? I need to talk with Whitney. We can meet back here in a couple of hours," I said.

The chief was reaching for his hat. "No problem Jake, keep your head down and don't leave this building without one of us with you."

The chief's reference to keeping my head down caused a moment that happened a few months back to flash through my mind, when I'd narrowly escaped sure death in the form of a 7MM rifle slug. That same chill ran up and down my spine just as it did that day.

I found Whitney in the small dispatch center for the PD. She'd easily made friends with the dispatcher and clerk. They were all talking as if they were lifelong friends rather than newly formed acquaintances. I just leaned on the door frame leading into the room and listened for several minutes. I wished that I didn't have to interrupt; I wished that none of this had happened. Whitney deserved to be happy right now instead of having to be worried for our safety. I was about to become very unpopular.

Chapter 20

"Nothing, you found nothing else?" exclaimed Blaine Alexander.

"I'm really at a loss too," stated Trooper Jarvis as he shrugged his shoulders.

"I've been part of search and rescues like this many times but with the way this is playin' out, it's as if we have to throw the book out the window. Nothing makes sense," said a fatigued Blaine as he sat back in his chair and placed his forehead in the palm of his right hand.

"It seems that every clue is pointing at the river, that Spaulding went into the water. If that's so, where'd he go?" snapped Trooper Jarvis.

"Spaulding goes off fishing and his daypack with what supplies he had with him was found near the riverbank. Spark follows his trail to the river and that's it. Spark then locates his fishing rod and net near the bank a short distance downriver from the daypack. No other sign has been found by the search teams, aircraft or Spark," recounted Blaine.

"From what everyone's said, Spaulding was familiar with the area. He seemed fine and was in good health," added Trooper Jarvis.

Blaine stood up and talked while pacing the room. "You know this has felt really odd from the beginning. If he'd drowned, then in my experience the body would've been discovered floating by now. At the very least some of his gear or clothing should've surfaced, don't you think?"

Trooper Jarvis eyed Blaine. "I agree – it's as if he doesn't want to be found."

Blaine turned and faced Trooper Jarvis. "Or, someone else doesn't want him to be found."

"That would mean . . ?"

"That's right; this is no accident. I believe we have to consider that possibility," said Blaine.

"Okay Blaine, I'm with you but I need to let Spark rest; he's not going to be much help at the moment. He's worked hard today and is spent."

"No Problem. I was able to reach Trooper Kramer in King Salmon. He knows where things stand. There's a team of a dozen search and rescue pros from Wasilla that should be here tonight. They're part of a mountain rescue team and they have connections to some additional K-9's that are more for finding cadavers than for tracking. I believe we need to begin looking for a body and hope for the best. More importantly, I think we need to expand our search area to include the shoreline of Aleknagik Lake."

"All right Blaine, I'm gonna pack it in for the night. I'll be up early and we can begin lining this out and then set things into motion once these mountain rescue guys arrive."

"Sure thing. In the mean time I'm gonna re-direct some of the search crews to begin a systematic search of the entire shoreline of the lake in hopes of finding something to go on. This is a huge lake but if my hunch is right, I think there should be some sign of a boat landing or human presence close to or on the shore and if that's the case we can narrow down our search area," explained Blaine.

Chuck Jones was getting fairly bored with this whole thing – impatient would be more like it. He'd spent his entire life being patient, waiting for the opportune moment. That's exactly how he's stayed alive and unconnected to his crimes for so many years.

Jones had seen a hundred or more hotshots who thought they could do what he did for a living. He's seen so many come and go that he's lost count. They're either not cut out for the work or they become careless and impatient, and are killed or at the very least caught.

Usually the targets that he's paid to take out realize they're targets. It's not that simple to just walk up and put a bullet in their head or take them out when they come out of their home in the morning. Nothing could be farther from the truth, the stark reality of the way things worked. Constant planning and patience alone make you persevere in this business. Being successful means staying alive and he's always been successful and doesn't intend on changing his ways.

He found where that VPSO lived. Dumbass Rohn sent Baxter a text about Blaine Alexander and a picture to boot. It was easy enough to see right on Baxter's phone. That's the sort of stupid shit that will get a person killed. He tried to access the voicemail associated with the phone but he needed the password to hear any messages.

He staked out the VPSO's house as long as he safely could without fear of being detected. It didn't seem that Rohn had returned and he saw no reason to chance confronting the VPSO. That would be far too risky.

Now he's fishing again. Normally he'd think this was perfect. He was even planning in his mind an actual fishing trip to this country next spring or summer. But he needed to get back to what he was so good at.

There had been some additional activity in Aleknagik with searchers going to that lodge where that fisherman had become lost. He believed that was pretty much holding the attention of the locals and he could move about fairly unnoticed but he knew he still needed to be cautious.

His mind was made up; he would return to Dillingham and get some food, maybe go to a restaurant or bar and just listen to what was being said. He wanted to know if Baxter's body had been discovered. He needed to get on with his plan so that he could be paid the money owed to him and then retire for good.

Jones walked slowly toward the old pickup he'd been driving since he arrived in Dillingham.

'Stupid fuckers, you could get anything from anybody if you waved enough green in front of their face.'

With that, Jones got into and started up his recent purchase and began the forty-five minute drive to Dillingham from the tiny community of Aleknagik.

Chapter 21

I stayed the night at the transient quarters available at the PD. The accommodations were meager and a bit noisy due to the traffic at the PD and attached jail but the bunk I chose was comfortable. The space had two beds, a full bath, microwave, sink, refrigerator and a small table. Since Whitney and I returned to Dillingham, the chief wouldn't allow us to leave the PD without him or one of his officers being with us. I put up a mild argument that such measures weren't necessary but the chief told me it was *'his town'* and *'his rules.'* I gave in rather quickly to the chief's demands. It sucked having to wait for an escort to go anywhere but I kept reminding myself that it was necessary to ensure my safety.

Getting Whitney on that plane the previous evening was pure hell. It was similar to trying to get a cat into a tub of water minus the scratch marks, though I thought a couple times Whitney was going to dig her claws into my face – well, her nails actually.

In the end, Whitney gave in and at least she told me she understood that it was best for her to return to Anchorage while I stayed behind and hopefully put an end to this mess before anyone else was hurt or killed.

I know she worried about me. I felt so bad for Whitney that I told her of the plans I had for our real honeymoon in Hawaii. I couldn't keep it secret any longer. Once again, I was willing to do anything to ensure she was content; she was my world after all.

Before I got the day underway, I decided to call Whitney.

"How was your trip back to Anchorage?" I asked once Whitney answered the phone.

"It was fine; Mark met me at the airport and drove me to my parents' place."

"I wanted to call and tell you hello and that I love you before things get too crazy here today."

Whitney was silent.

"Baby, I'm really sorry things happened this way. If I could undo it I would – but I can't. Glenn being killed and you being in danger is just too much. I know we should be together and we will be. Mark gave me forty-eight hours to figure this out and that's exactly what I plan to do. For everyone's sake, this has to end now," I said almost apologetically.

"Dammit Jacob Rohn . . ."

Whitney began but stopped. I could tell she was beginning to cry; I could hear her voice cracking.

"I'll call you later today. If you need me but can't reach me, don't panic. The cell service out here isn't that great. Call Mark if you need anything."

"Okay Jacob. Promise you'll be careful." Whitney sobbed.

Man, my heart couldn't break into many more pieces. Hearing her like that was too much, sheer torture. I had to hang up before I lost it too.

"I'll be careful. I love you Whitney."

"I love you too Jacob."

After ending my call to Whitney I called Mark.

"Thanks for ensuring Whitney was safe. You know I owe you for that," I said when Mark answered.

"Look Jake, that's what we do – take care of each other. If we don't look out for each other then who would?"

Mark was right.

"Nothing new to report here Mark. I was just about to go grab a bite and then meet up with Chief Perry," I said.

Mark cleared his throat. "I've been thinking about this. Since this asshole is probably trying to blend in with every other visitor in Dillingham, why don't we plant someone to do the same thing? Blend in, hang out. Maybe hear or see something."

"Sounds like a good idea but look what happened to Baxter. We don't need a repeat of that...who'd you have in mind?" I asked.

"Barry Simms, that son-of-a-gun would fit right in out there."

Barry was a lifelong Alaskan, born in Anchorage. He had five or six years with the Anchorage PD before coming to work as an investigator in our unit. He could probably act the least like a cop than any of us. Barry could be described as the quintessential Alaskan male; he liked fishing and hunting and possessed a fun side to him that would make him ideal for undercover work.

"I think that's a good plan."

Mark chuckled. "I'm glad you agree because he should be there within the hour or even sooner. He was scheduled to fly out on the first flight of the day to Dillingham. I arranged a rental car for him. Did you know there were only two places to rent a car in Dillingham and they only have maybe a dozen or so cars anyway?"

"Yeah I know. Chief Perry already contacted them and all the rentals were accounted for and checked out. I thought maybe our killer rented a car but I guess not.

We are curious how he's getting around," I explained.

"Oh, okay, that was a good idea. Barry's instructions are to get there, blend in as a fisherman and see what he can find out. If you need to contact him I would suggest texting him…at least that was what I told him you would do. He should be letting you know when he arrives. Is there anything else before I go?" Mark asked.

"Well, Chief Perry has requested passenger manifests from all the airlines for a period of twenty-four hours before and after my arrival. I expect to get that in the next day or so. Also, the crime scene investigators returned to Anchorage last night. They were on Whitney's flight."

"I saw Jeff Fleener and spoke with him at the airport. He seemed confident that if you get the right donor – he has enough DNA evidence to match it to the killer, he's gonna start processing it, but unlike T.V., it'll be several days before he can compare the results to databases of known samples," Mark explained.

"Sounds good Mark; I need to get moving – I'm hungry and I plan on meeting Chief Perry in a little while back here at the PD."

"Alright Jake, watch your top knot!"

As I hung up the phone I couldn't help but wonder. Mark always says that. *'Watch your top knot.'* What in the hell is a top knot anyway?

Within maybe thirty minutes I received a text message. It was from Barry Simms.

'Jake I just arrived, waiting for my car now. I have a room at a B&B. Until I hear differently, I'll be looking about town for anything suspicious - bs.'

Simple enough. I replied to Barry letting him know that I didn't have anything to add and to check in every couple of hours, at least. Oh, and to watch his top knot.

Chapter 22

Blaine Alexander had just completed a briefing to all the volunteer searchers that were part of the now massive effort that included three aircraft, five K-9's and at least a hundred individuals. The arrival of that mountain rescue group and their resources was a definite boost to the combined effort.

It had been three days since Ronald Spaulding left the Chesterfield Lodge on foot, to go fishing. The only sign of him since that time had been his daypack and fishing gear that were found along the Agulowak River a mile or so from the lodge.

The aircraft have continued their systematic grid search patterns over an area more than twenty miles square. Three K-9's and at least three dozen searchers were meticulously working their way around the entire lake shore looking for the slightest sign of Spaulding or any human encroachment that could be found and investigated.

The other two K-9's, including Trooper Jarvis, and volunteers were expanding their ground search on both sides of the Agulowak River between the lodge and Aleknagik Lake. It was helpful that the smattering of real pros from the mountain search group brought their knowledge of how people react when they'd become lost, hurt and disoriented. Mixed in with the expert knowledge about the terrain and local influences the hometown searchers could provide, it was the perfect recipe to find something that would lead them to Spaulding.

Blaine and Chase Rayburn were left alone in the main lodge's fireplace and sitting room which had turned into the headquarters for the operation.

Chase could sense that Blaine was quite sullen and fatigued. "Blaine, you're doing a great job at managing this search."

Blaine turned to the lodge manager. "Thanks for the support Chase. Everyone here at the Chesterfield has been quite helpful – not only in assisting in searching but helping keep this group of people fed and allowing them to crash in vacant rooms or anywhere a cot can be set up when they need the rest."

"If I was lost, I'd want you in charge of looking for me," added Chase.

Blaine smiled. "It's not me Chase; I answer to the troopers and they answer to the statewide search and rescue coordinator. It works because everyone involved puts forth a good effort and exchange ideas. All I'm doing is keeping track of where everyone goes, maintaining the supplies and praying that no one else gets lost or injured in the process."

"Well, just the same; I'm telling you that you're the one seeing to it that everyone does all they can to find Spaulding. How's his family doing?" asked Chase.

Blaine pursed his lips together tightly. "His family - I haven't spoken to any of them. I know Trooper Kramer's been keeping in touch with his wife. Now, that has to be a tough thing to cope with; I'm not sure I could handle talking to Spaulding's family."

What if it was his family member that was lost? What would he do? Blaine just hung his head and wondered silently if there was anything more that he could do to help find Spaulding.

Search team twelve-alpha consisted of one K-9 and handler, four ground searchers and a boat operator. They'd been searching the shoreline along the very eastern end of Aleknagik Lake in an area referred to as Sunshine Valley. It was mid-afternoon; the water on the lake was choppy. The wind had come up and increased in intensity as the day wore on. They stopped and ate their lunch a little while earlier. The team had been methodically searching the shoreline and the shallows of the lake for any sign of Spaulding.

They'd stopped their boat and checked the bank at least fifty different times already. Whenever they spotted anything that looked as if a person had landed a boat on the shore or even walked on the shore they would exit their own craft and conduct a thorough search of the area.

Thus far they found a few camping spots, areas where wood had been gathered or anglers had been fishing, but nothing that would lead them to Spaulding. They even checked areas on the shore that simply appeared to be easily accessible from the water but still came up empty.

They were assigned a five mile area of shoreline to search and were nearing the end of that mission. One of the spotters pointed out a sandy area where the lake was fairly shallow along the shore. In the sand you could see the tell-tale marks the 'V' shape of a boat hull leaves as it is pulled into the shallows and in this case also onto the sandy and muddy bank.

This was just the sort of indicator they'd seen and checked out many times already throughout the day. A boat had been pulled up part-way onto the shore and, judging by the tracks on the bank, someone had exited the boat and apparently made multiple trips to the brush ten feet from the waterline.

As they'd done previously, the K-9 took the lead and the ground searchers spread out up and down the bank to look for any tracks or other signs of human presence. The K-9 was acting differently on this occasion, almost pulling his handler into the brush to a spot maybe thirty yards from the lake.

When these types of dogs are trained to find a body or person, they give a sign to their handler that they've hit pay dirt; that they've found what they were trained to find. To the K-9 it's just an exercise to get praise from their trainer, to get a treat. Go forth and find it and then bark, howl, scratch or simply sit there until their human recognizes they found it and wait for the commendation to follow.

That's exactly what happened. That finely tuned animal instantly began scratching and sniffing at the ground. He sat and began to whine – he was letting his handler know he found it and he wanted his praise and treat for the effort.

The handler immediately noticed the freshly turned soil and leaves on the ground of what he thought could be a shallow grave, but the dead giveaway was a human hand that was protruding from the dirt and vegetation. Animals had apparently unearthed and partially devoured flesh from the hand and left it visible for search team twelve-alpha to discover.

Chapter 23

I decided to go to the local market and get myself some food to hold me over. Like any good cop, I was hoping the chief would buy me lunch at one of the town's eateries later in the day. I knew the chief didn't want me to be moving about on my own but I decided I could get to the store and back before the chief arrived at his office. There wasn't an officer available to accompany me and I was just too famished to wait any longer. Later on I'll let him know I made the brief trip alone but had been cautious and remained wary of my surroundings.

I wanted to tread lightly with Chief Perry due to the circumstances. Since I didn't work for the man I could do whatever I pleased but that wasn't how to handle the situation. The fact is I wanted something to eat and I felt it was better to beg for forgiveness rather than ask for permission.

There were two grocery stores to choose from. I chose the one closest to the department. I was hungry.

I found the dairy case and picked a pint of chocolate milk from the shelf and was making my way to the bread aisle in hopes of finding a suitable treat to accompany the milk. Just as I made it to the bakery section and had decided what to select, I heard a cell phone begin to ring, well ring wasn't the correct word but it was clearly sounding off; the tune was unmistakably the Hawaii 5-0 theme song. I knew that ring tone and that the owner of the phone that played it was dead.

If Baxter's phone was now in the possession his killer, the killer had the clear advantage. He knew who I was and I'm sure he knew what I looked like but I didn't have a clue what he might look like even though I suspected he was a male and was alone – but in reality I couldn't be absolutely sure.

I immediately realized that taking a chance and venturing away from the PD alone wasn't a very smart move on my part. Just in the next aisle was quite possibly the man whose mission was to end my life.

I'd been vigilant during my brief drive to the store and though I'd seen others in the store I didn't notice anyone who seemed suspicious or who would begin to meet the ideal description I had in mind of my potential assassin. This was bad news. I was struggling with what I should do next. Should I draw my weapon and charge around the aisle and confront...uh...who? What if there were other people in the aisle or what if the person I'm looking for already moved on? What if it's just a coincidence and some little old lady is talking on the phone to her grandkids and I scare her to death? Shit! What's my next move?

It might have seemed like hours after I heard the phone ring but in reality it was just a few seconds. I looked around and behind me along the wall was a door marked *'office'*. I quickly walked to the door, tried the knob and it turned. I pulled open the door and stepped inside.

A tiny, frail man of maybe fifty years was seated at desk in the office. He looked up at me but before he could say a word I held up my badge and introduced myself. That seemed to settle the gentleman down because the color instantly returned to his face.

"Sir, I'm so sorry to bother you but let me explain," I began.

In just a couple minutes I had the store employee, who turned out to be the day manager, up to speed with what he needed to know. His name was Mr. Foster and was more than willing to help however he could.

At about that moment my own phone rang; it was Mark Dillon.

"Hi Mark, you're not going to believe what just happened."

"You're not going to believe what I just did; I'm such an idiot sometimes. I started to call you but dialed Glenn Baxter's phone instead. Imagine my surprise if someone answered. How creepy is that?" explained Mark.

"Mark, we didn't recover Glenn's phone."

"Oh, I guess I didn't realize that – where is it?" Mark asked.

"That's just it; I just heard Glenn's phone ringing, here in one of the grocery stores – you heard it before yourself. When it rings his phone plays the Hawaii 5-0 theme. Not even two minutes ago I heard it ringing right here in this very grocery store where I stopped to buy myself some breakfast."

It was clear that Mark hadn't connected all the dots yet. "Okay, so who has Glenn's phone then?"

I had to start over but I explained to Mark that the scene investigation of Glenn's death didn't produce Glenn's phone. We suspected that the killer took it and from information on the phone he found out my connection to VPSO Alexander and had staked out his home.

"My fault Mark; I guess I failed to tell you that Glenn's phone was missing and our suspicions are that his killer took it."

"No shit! You just heard the phone ringing at about the same time I accidentally called it. You talk about a lucky break; did you see who had it?" Mark excitedly asked.

"No I didn't. I was in a really tough spot so I ducked into the store office but I have a couple of things to check; let me call you back," at which point I hung up the phone before Mark could drill me as to why I didn't jump the bastard.

After hanging up I turned to Mr. Foster. "I see security cameras in the store; please tell me you have a security system recording in some manner - that I'm able to review the last few minutes of what was recorded."

Mr. Foster really perked up. "As a matter of fact we have a great digital system that was just upgraded a couple of months ago. Twelve color cameras that record twenty-four hours a day."

Mr. Foster got out of his chair and walked over to the back wall and opened up two large closet doors exposing a shelf with two huge computer monitors. Each monitor screen was split up in six equal parts showing what the twelve different cameras were recording at that very moment. There was a keyboard and hard drive system on a shelf below the monitors.

I could see on one of the monitors the very location I'd been just minutes before when I heard Baxter's phone. There was no one there or in the adjacent aisle. Whoever had that phone had moved along.

"Mr. Foster – if this works as good as it looks, you're gonna be a hero."

Within minutes Mr. Foster was showing me how the very simple interface of the system worked. One monitor was changed to a view of all twelve cameras at once and continued showing the live feed. The second monitor was utilized to review recorded footage from any combination of the twelve cameras. It was simple to locate the time stamp when I was standing in the bread section. I elected to review just one camera stream on the monitor.

The camera angle clearly showed me in my aisle standing there - about to select my food from the shelf and the aisle where I heard the phone ring. A man was clearly seen walking up the adjacent aisle moving toward the camera. When he was about even with me he suddenly stopped and reached into his shirt pocket and unmistakably removed a phone and looked at it. He returned the phone to his pocket, abruptly turned and went back the way he'd come from which was toward the front of the store where the exit was located.

As the man stopped, he was facing the camera and actually looked up and directly at the camera for a brief instant before turning away.

"Mr. Foster, can we pause this at any position?" I asked.

Mr. Foster came to my side. "Sure, let me show you."

Much like a DVD, Mr. Foster showed me how I was able to pause the footage, rewind and go forward in slow motion. It took a couple of tries to get it right but I was able to stop that beautifully clear picture at the exact moment when the man was looking squarely at the camera.

"How can I save or copy this?" I asked.

Mr. Foster had all the right answers. "Well, we can print it directly to our printer. If you prefer we can save it as a photo file and we can also save any section of video that you want."

I knew that video surveillance had advanced and became more affordable. This system was fantastic. It didn't record sound but I wasn't about to complain about that.

I saved the video of the man walking up the aisle, looking at the phone and then walking away. I saved and printed full length and close-up photos of the same man. It took a few more minutes of searching camera angles to follow the man as he entered the store and walked directly to that aisle and as soon as the phone rang, he walked right back out of the store. I was able to save that as video also. It was apparent that he hadn't ever been in a position to see me while he was in the store.

Maybe he was following me; maybe it was just coincidence. There weren't any cameras that showed the parking lot or anything outside the store except for the front entrance itself.

Once again I needed Mr. Foster's help. "Do you carry jump drives in the store?"

Without answering, Mr. Foster opened a desk drawer and retrieved a small USB storage device and gave it to me. "Keep it Mr. Rohn."

I thanked Mr. Foster, gathered up my photos and after saving the video and images to the jump drive I turned to Mr. Foster with one final request. "Will it be okay if I sit tight for a little while? I need to make a few phone calls."

My first call was to Chief Perry. I explained to him what had happened. At first he thought I was screwing with him.

"No way; you're messin' with my head so early in the day. What in the hell are you doing by yourself? I thought I was clear on what my rules were about your safety. Dammit Rohn, you may not work for me but this is my town and being responsible for everyone's safety includes you, like it or not!"

"Yes chief, it happened just like I said it did. Can you believe such luck and I have photos of this guy – I know he's the one who killed Baxter and is after me. We're gonna nail his ass to the wall," I boldly predicted.

I purposely ignored the chief's anger concerning me leaving the PD alone. What could I say; I screwed up and didn't want to admit it. Chief Perry knew I heard his message loud and clear.

"Alright Rohn, I'd heard you could be a joker at times but I don't think this is the right time for that sort of crap. What do you want me to do?"

"I'm not joking. First I think it would be best that you come over to where I am; maybe you can look at a photo I have and make sure this guy isn't just waiting for me to leave the store," I suggested.

Chief Perry agreed. "Alright, I'll be there in a few minutes."

I ended that call and immediately called Mark Dillon. He picked up right where I had earlier cut him off.

"What do you mean hangin' up on me, I need to know what's happening Rohn."

"Mark, that's what I'm calling you about. I've good news for once."

The prospect of good news seemingly struck a positive chord with Mark; I knew he was worried about my safety and of course the potential of an additional butt chewing he may get because of my actions.

After a brief silence, Mark spoke. "Good news; now I like the sound of that."

So I told Mark about the surveillance video and the photos of our suspect I was able to print out and save to a floppy drive.

"I should be able to get these emailed to you fairly quickly; Chief Perry's on his way to meet me. We're gonna get these photos to his men and see if we can find this guy before it's too late and he gets to me or gets out of town should he get spooked or think we're on to him," I explained to Mark.

"When I get these photos I'll distribute them to every agency I can think of, maybe we'll get lucky and get an ID on this joker," suggested Mark.

As I hung up with Mark, there was a light knock on the door. It was Chief Perry.

Mr. Foster let him into the office.

I handed Chief Perry the best close-up photo I had printed of the suspect. "Do you recognize him?"

The chief looked over the photo and finally spoke. "No, this guy is new to me. You're positive this is our suspect?"

"Ninety-nine percent sure chief; the circumstances would be just too coincidental. Since you don't recognize this photo, I'd guess he's new to town."

"I didn't see this guy near the store. Let's get to the PD and I'll call my officers in. We'll give each of them a copy of these photos and have them start beating the bushes and locate this guy," said the chief.

As we started out of the store it dawned on me I hadn't eaten. Damn, I was hungry.

Chapter 24

"SAR base, this is search team twelve-alpha."

It was scratchy but the voice was clear enough to understand on the handheld VHF radio Blaine was monitoring at the search base.

Blaine spent the day receiving and documenting information from the various search teams and aircraft that were completing their missions. Some of the information was provided to him over the radio and some in person. The message was becoming redundant: current assignment accomplished with negative results, awaiting further orders.

Many of the teams and aircraft were provided with new instructions; others returned to the lodge to rest and replenish supplies before continuing their search.

Trooper Jarvis already returned and was with the VPSO in the temporary search headquarters.

Blaine stood and walked in the direction of the radio. "Sounds like another search team has finished. I guess we'll bring them in. It's getting late in the day and I know they need a break."

Trooper Jarvis nodded in approval.

Blaine keyed the push to talk button on the radio. "This is SAR base, go ahead twelve-alpha."

The radio crackled and again the voice emitting from the speaker was scratchy but certainly clear enough to be understood. "Twelve-alpha requesting troopers and VPSO Alexander to respond to our location, area twelve."

Blaine looked at the map. "That's Sunshine Valley, maybe a twenty minute boat ride from the lodge." With little hesitation Blaine once again keyed the radio. "We're on our way, ETA twenty minutes."

"Ten-four, twelve-alpha standing by."

Blaine didn't even have to ask; Trooper Jarvis was on his feet and headed to the door. "Let's go."

Blaine knew what this meant: a search team radioing in and are unwilling to say what they've found over the air. The news can't be good. Requesting trooper response too; that had him baffled though. It had to be dreadful news; that was a certainty.

It was perhaps twenty-five minutes later when VPSO Alexander and Trooper Jarvis arrived at search team twelve-alpha's location. They'd landed their boat at the extreme east end of the lake at Sunshine Valley.

Blaine immediately called to the team leader and spoke with him in private. The remainder of the search team and Trooper Jarvis stayed with the boats.

After several moments, Blaine started toward the brush with the team leader and waved to Trooper Jarvis inviting him to join them. The trio entered the woods and in less than a hundred feet they were standing at the edge of an apparent makeshift grave. A human hand protruded up from the seemingly soft dirt.

"The million dollar question," began Trooper Jarvis. "Is this Ronald Spaulding?"

Blaine spoke up. "The grave seems fresh enough. It's hard to tell how old the corpse is but I don't know of anyone else missing around here except Spaulding."

Trooper Jarvis was thinking out loud. "The flesh on the hand has been chewed on by animals but I'd guess the body is reasonably fresh, hard to say for sure but in that condition it would have to be less than a week old."

"There's nothing we can see that tells us for sure but I think we need to get in touch with Trooper Kramer to get this passed along up the chain of command and wait for direction," suggested Blaine.

"I agree with you Blaine. We need to secure this area and wait for investigators to arrive and extract the body, preserve any evidence and positively identify it as Spaulding," said Trooper Jarvis.

"Alright," said the search team leader. "Look, I'm no detective – but if this is Spaulding, he's ten miles or more from where his daypack was found. The bigger question is how in the hell did he get here in the first place?"

"Yeah, you're right but the next question is who's responsible for this?" said Trooper Jarvis. "Spaulding or not, we have a homicide on our hands."

It was at least an hour later that Blaine and Trooper Jarvis reached Aleknagik. Before leaving the crime scene, Blaine had arranged for a couple of the mountain rescue searchers to camp on the shore near where the body had been found in order to preserve the site of the horrific find. They were always prepared to stay out in the elements; this would be a piece of cake compared to some of the cold weather and mountain searches they'd been a part of. Blaine and Trooper Jarvis left instructions for all remaining teams to remain at the lodge once they returned.

Blaine used a phone at the State Parks office to call Trooper Kramer in King Salmon.

"Hi Donny, I'm in Aleknagik with Trooper Jarvis. We have an update and a dilemma."

Trooper Kramer was listening intently. "Go ahead Blaine, what do you have?"

VPSO Alexander explained the findings to Donny Kramer.

"Donny, what do you think we should do, I mean as far as the search goes?"

Trooper Kramer was quiet for a few moments, obviously formulating a plan. "Okay, you have the scene secured; I'll notify headquarters and can assume a team of investigators will be on their way out there fairly quick. Did you get the areas searched that you set out to get done today?"

"Yeah," answered Blaine.

"I'm going to call the captain and the statewide search and rescue coordinator for some guidance regarding the search. I have an idea on what to do but it's best to let them make the final decision. At least for now, all of the search teams are back at the lodge awaiting additional instructions, correct?" asked Trooper Kramer.

"Yeah, that's the orders we gave before we left for Aleknagik. The aircraft had already returned to Dillingham and most of the searchers were at the lodge but the few that hadn't arrived there were in radio contact and had been called back," said Blaine.

"Okay then, good work guys. I'll call you as soon as I speak with the bosses and let you know what they say. Is your cell number good?"

"Yeah," said Blaine.

With that, Blaine disconnected with Trooper Kramer and filled in Trooper Jarvis on what he'd been told.

"What do you say about heading back to Dillingham and getting some food and then waiting to hear from Donny?" suggested Trooper Jarvis.

"Why not? My cell phone won't work at the lodge anyway and Donny will need to reach us fairly soon most likely," Blaine said as they headed for his vehicle to begin the trip to Dillingham.

Chapter 25

The chief followed me over to the PD; knowing what the suspect we were looking for looked like was a good thing. Not knowing how he was getting around and that little bit of doubt whether we were even onto the right person made me keep all my senses on high alert.

By the time I met up with the chief, he'd already called in all of his officers and they were beginning to assemble in the tiny squad room.

The chief elected to keep his normal guys scheduled for patrol duty in uniform. The rest of the men were in plain clothes. While we waited for everyone to arrive, I emailed Mark the files I'd saved from the security system. I then utilized the chief's computer and printed several copies of both the full length and close-up photos of our suspect.

The suspect in the photo had the appearance of a rugged outdoorsman. He was over six foot tall, white with no facial hair. His hair was a dirty blonde color and was long enough to be pulled back and kept in a pony tail that hung well below his shoulders in the center of his back. He was wearing a camouflaged jacket, carhart pants and boots.

His mannerisms suggested confidence. He looked to be middle to late forties.

Once everyone was seated, I began the briefing.

"Everyone knows we're looking for the killer of Glenn Baxter. It's believed the same murderer may have been hired to kill me; this goes back to a prior case I was involved in that cost a heavy player in Denver a lot of money over drugs. I've passed out two photos to each of you. This man is our suspect. These pictures were taken by the security camera at Ginger's Grocery earlier today."

One of the officers looked at me and asked a logical question. "How do we know this guy is who we are looking for?"

I would have asked the same thing. "Good question. Glenn Baxter's phone wasn't recovered at the murder scene and this suspect has been connected directly to that phone."

I was glad that explanation sufficed and I didn't have to answer how we connected him to that phone. I looked over the group of officers who were each busy looking at the photos and obviously processing the information they were getting.

"What about the airport? Have you given these to TSA?" asked another officer.

The chief answered that question. "I spoke to the head of security at the airport previously and made him aware of this fugitive but I've since contacted him and was able to send him digital images of this suspect so that they can be on the lookout for him."

After the chief concluded, I continued. "I'm curious if any of you know this man by chance or may recognize his face from seeing him somewhere in town the past few days?"

As I expected the responses were all negative.

"Okay, what the chief and I are asking is that you keep this information confidential and you uniformed officers keep your eyes peeled and make an extra effort to cover every area in town you possibly can in hopes that this suspect may be spotted. Those of you in plain clothes should go into stores, bars and shops – everywhere you can think of and try and spot this guy. No one should confront him; he's most likely a trained professional and to preserve his own safety he won't hesitate to kill any of you if he feels trapped or threatened. Notify the chief or myself as quickly as possible if you spot him. Are we all clear on this?" I asked.

I know cops; most of us think of ourselves as being invincible. A young cop I once knew called it having an 'S' on our chest – with good on our side, we were supermen. The smart cop thinks about this kind of situation and knows that safety comes from being properly informed, trained and prepared. I observed my audience nodding their heads in agreement with what I'd been saying. They all responded in the affirmative to my question which was what I was hoping for from this group of men.

Chief Perry had been listening intently but felt he needed to let his men know this was his town.

The chief stood up. "Guys, do any of you have any questions about this or what your assignments are?"

Again the group responded that they understood.

The chief shook his head up and down. "Alright, let's get to it and call with anything to report."

The officers filed out of the squad room and headed off to catch a killer. These men were young and eager, but with that youthfulness there's inexperience.

After everyone had left I turned to the chief. "What do you think – lunch?"

The chief grabbed his hat and aimed for the door. "Good idea, you're buying!"

On the drive over to the restaurant I called Barry Simms. We thought it best if he didn't meet us at the PD to ensure his cover remained intact. I explained to him what had happened earlier and that I had some photos of our suspect for him. We decided to leave the photos at the front counter of the restaurant in an envelope; he could pick them up later. Barry filled me in on what he'd been doing but didn't have any progress to report; perhaps these photos will be a help to him.

It was comical once we entered the restaurant. Two grown men jockeying for position to be the one with his back to the wall and facing the door; for some reason cops always have to be facing the door. It's not something you are taught in the academy or even in your training. It has to be something of a learned instinct – I can't say I have any other real explanation for the phenomenon.

"Hey chief if I'm buying, I get the first pick of seats. You're just going to have to trust me to watch the door and have your back – that's the rule."

Chief Perry gave in and agreed. I'm not sure if he trusted me that much or was just a cheapskate and didn't want to buy lunch. Probably the latter I decided.

"What's good here?" I asked.

"Everything – the meatloaf sandwich for the lunch special is what I'm having."

I thought it over and went for the club sandwich instead.

We ate pretty much in silence but as I was finishing lunch my phone rang. Mark

Dillon's name and the picture of a monkey popped up on the caller ID.

Okay, the monkey thing was an inside joke.

"What's going on Mark?"

"The guy you are looking for is dead," Mark said.

"Dead!" I blurted into the phone. "How could that happen and how could you know so damn fast?"

Mark knew he had me going. "Hold your horses there cowboy; what I'm saying is the government says this guy died twenty years ago in a car bombing that happened over in Europe."

I was speechless; a dead guy is after me and killed Baxter! "Back up Mark, normally you are the clueless one but I'm not following."

"Let me explain," said Mark. "I sent those photos you emailed me everywhere I could think of. I know this FBI instructor in Quantico, at the FBI academy; he was able to feed them into this facial recognition software they have and it spit out the name of this guy that was killed in Europe."

"But," I started.

Mark ignored my attempt to interject. "He won't give me all the details but this person is a German national who grew up in the U.S. He was recruited by our government for some classified reason but he was killed in Europe. That's pretty much all he would tell me. He didn't seem too interested in this guy but wanted to let me know how dangerous he is and that we needed to…"

"I know Mark, watch our top knot. How sure could he be that this was the same person?"

"If you'd let me finish, I was gonna say be careful but top knot works too. To answer your question, he said this technology was maybe ninety-five percent accurate," Mark concluded.

"You're telling me this is a government trained killer of some sort that murdered Baxter and is now gunning for me?" I know I was white as a ghost at the thought of such a man hired to kill me.

"Apparently this is fairly common. These guys swap sides or go out on their own to pursue the American dream. In this case he figures this chap freelances as a gun for hire, hit man, for whoever pays the most cash. Just so you know, I would expect black helicopters over Dillingham within a few hours. Unknowingly, I think you've stumbled onto something big."

"Are you shittin' me Mark?"

"Actually I am; it feels good too. What he really told me was to keep him informed of our progress in apprehending this guy whose real name is Johan Frank."

"Alright Mark, we have everyone here looking for this joker and I've filled in Barry as well. We'll contact everyone and pass along this new information and will let you know what turns up."

"Okay Jake, sounds like a good plan. Now I need to go see Julie with this. Oh and Jake . . ."

"Yeah?"

"Watch your top knot!" Mark said almost laughingly.

Cop humor – if not for a way to relieve stress I think we all would be ate up with ulcers.

After the bizarre and revealing phone call from Mark, I quietly filled in the chief on what I learned.

"We need to let all my men know," said the chief.

"Yeah, and Barry Simms," I added.

We left the restaurant and returned to the PD. The chief spent a couple of hours calling all his men and relaying the news about Johan Frank. I called Simms and brought him up to speed.

The chief entered the squad room and took a seat near the desk I was using. "Everyone knows what we know; they all have photos and specific direction not to try and take this guy alone. I damn sure hope no one comes across Frank and decides to be Mr. Hero; there are rules we're bound to follow. This guy has one rule, survive any way he possibly can!"

More time passed without any news. I wanted the chief and me to drive around town and help look for Frank but he suggested we stay put and keep checking in with all the eyes we had out there and to keep track of what had been completed and what needed to be.

I thought he was right. Moreover, if this guy saw me and either tried to kill me or got spooked – we could lose any chance we may have to capture him.

It was getting late and I wanted something more to eat. "Chief, how about we order up a few pizzas and all the guys can stop by a couple at a time and get a bite to eat."

"Okay, you get them ordered and I'll check in with everyone and let them know."

Since learning about the reputation of Baxter's killer, we'd doubled the patrols up, so we only had five units instead of ten. We thought it would be safer that way. Barry Simms was the exception; he was keeping in contact with me fairly regularly by text message so we knew where he was.

Just as I was about to order the pizza, VPSO Blaine Alexander and a trooper sauntered through the door of the PD.

I met Blaine and shook his hand. "Hi Blaine, how the hell is the search going for that missing fisherman?"

"Jake, do you know Trooper Jarvis?" asked Blaine just as the chief joined us.

"No I don't. Jake Rohn," I introduced myself and shook the trooper's hand. "This is Chief Perry."

After the introduction Blaine answered my question. "The search is why we're here Jake. We found a body but aren't quite sure what we have."

Chapter 26

I quickly passed my job of ordering pizzas over to the dispatcher on duty. I even added one to the order for Blaine and Trooper Jarvis. "Guys, let's go into the squad room and talk."

Blaine repeated the details of the search and rescue to the chief and me.

"The missing fisherman was found miles from where he was lost, buried in a shallow grave?" asked the chief.

"Well, maybe," replied Blaine.

"You have a body in a grave; you think it may be Spaulding but can't be sure until it's recovered and an ID is made?" I asked.

"Pretty much. I've called Trooper Kramer in King Salmon, this is his case. We have the scene secured and are waiting for additional orders from him," continued Blaine.

"Wow, that's some heavy shit," I said. "Wait until you hear about our latest bombshell."

I related to Blaine and Trooper Jarvis the events of our day. They already knew about Baxter's death but our recent discoveries took them by surprise just as it had us. "There's more though, Blaine; can I talk with you privately?"

We went into the chief's office and I sat on the edge of the desk before I spoke. "Blaine, I think this guy has been watching your home. We found signs that someone was staking it out and we think it was Baxter's killer. Since we believe he has Baxter's phone I guess he could've seen the information about you I sent to Baxter. I messed up. Your wife and family are with her mom."

Blaine listened intently. "I called Diane and she told me she was at her mom's but didn't say why. I'm glad you saw to my family's safety but it's not your fault that some nut may have been watching my home. Thanks for letting me know."

I hoped Blaine knew how I felt; family is sacred. I'd never intentionally put his at risk. I was glad he took it as well as he did.

After a few minutes of idle conversation Blaine and I joined the other two men in the squad room.

I gave Trooper Jarvis and Blaine the photos I had printed earlier. "Here are photos of the person we believe to be this Johan Frank character."

Blaine looked up at me while pointing at one of the pictures of Frank. "This is the guy?"

"Yeah it is," I said.

Blaine got excited then. "I saw this guy, when I first began working on this search. He was hanging around the boat launch at Aleknagik Lake; I spoke to him briefly. He seemed like a curious bystander – I told him a search was just getting under way for a missing fisherman. He asked if he could help . . . I let him help me load my boat with some supplies. Holy shit! I mean, I liked the guy. I thought what a nice person – up there probably fishing or something and was willing to throw in and help me out."

Chief Perry spoke up. "Have you seen him again?"

"No, not that I recall but there are almost always people near the landing this time of year. Many people fish there and of course the locals come and go to their homes on the shore across that part of the lake but the person I saw was no local," answered Blaine.

Blaine knew what he was talking about. There was one road that connected Dillingham to the community of Aleknagik. The road ended right at the boat launch where most locals that lived around that end of the lake parked their cars and made the final trek to their homes across the water by boat. About half of the small community was accessible by road and the other half was across that portion of the lake which narrowed down to the source and beginning of the Wood River that eventually flowed to Nushagak Bay at the mouth of the Nushagak River at Dillingham.

With the fishing and tourist season in full swing and hunting season right around the corner, the boat launch was certainly a focal point as it was the only public access to the lake directly at the end of the Lake Road as it was called.

I had formulated a plan. "It will be dark in a couple of hours. I'll have Barry Simms head out that way and see if he can see our guy at the lake. Barry likes to fish and he may spot this guy. Chief, can you have one of your plain clothes teams drive out there and poke around and be close in the event Barry needs help?"

We set the plan in motion – at the moment we could only wait. There wasn't much else to go on anyway.

Chuck Jones felt uncomfortable in Dillingham. He always felt closed in when it came to small towns. He thought there was a great deal more anonymity in larger cities. That damn phone of Baxter's ringing like it did almost made him piss himself. Imagine that, big bad killer pissing his pants – now that was funny.

He would do some more fishing and try to relax a bit. He didn't think Baxter's body had been discovered. Everyone was talking about that missing fisherman. He had so easily spoken to that cop who was loading his boat and heading out on that search. What would the big secret be anyway – the more people that knew about the missing man and helped look would be for best, he thought.

He'd driven by the trooper's office, the PD, and where the VPSO lived. There was nothing happening that had appeared out of the ordinary in his opinion, nor did he see any sign of Rohn. From his conversation with the employee at the charter service, tomorrow was the soonest Rohn would be back from that remote lake.

He sometimes longed for that life he missed out on, an existence where he didn't constantly have to look over his shoulder. Choices he made as a young man, looking for adventure and money. If there was only a way to go back in time and knock some sense into that adolescent who had such a bright and long future ahead of him! But no, this was reality.

'Suck it up and deal with it like you have been for so long now.'

He was better at doing his job than the cops around here were at stopping him from completing his work. He had nothing to be concerned about. Just as Jones thought that he'd caught the last fish of the day, he felt that familiar and wonderful tug on his fishing pole. A big grin replaced the scowl on Jones's face.

Chapter 27

Barry Simms stopped by the restaurant where, earlier that day, Rohn had left the envelope containing pictures of Johan Frank character. He took the time to enjoy a hot meal while he had the opportunity and was very happy that he did. Not long afterwards, Rohn called him and directed him to Aleknagik Lake. It was a long shot but there was a chance that Frank might be at the lake. Rohn was fairly confident that Frank had been seen there a few days before and, strange as it might seem, it was believed he'd been fishing. Not what you would expect from some big time hit man. Maybe this was just one big wild goose chase.

Simms didn't mind the trip to Aleknagik. He'd taken the time to drive out earlier that day just to check it out. The lake was incredible. He did remember people coming and going frequently at the lake, but didn't really notice anything he thought warranted a closer look.

He brought his fishing gear to Dillingham in order to help pass himself off as another tourist getting in on some of the fantastic fishing in the area. Maybe he'd get a chance to *'wet a line'* as he referred to fishing.

Simms knew that a plainclothes patrol consisting of two officers from the Dillingham PD was his back up if needed and should be at or near the lake by now. He hadn't met them but Rohn provided him a detailed enough description and thought they should be easy enough to pick out.

Simms arrived at the end of the Lake Road and parked in one of the few empty spaces available close to the water. A group of fishermen were busy loading a boat at the ramp and three people were spread out along the lake shore, fishing.

'Dammit,' Simms swore under his breath. *'I should've brought some field glasses so that I could get a closer look at these guys who are fishing.'*

He was there to fish too, so he grabbed up his gear and walked down to the lake and began a routine of casting a lure into the water and slowly retrieving it.

In a casual manner, Simms studied all the people at the boat launch. None of them was the man he was searching for. He knew he could eventually maneuver himself close enough to get a good look at the other fishermen in order to determine whether or not any of them was Johan Frank.

Simms laughed to himself. He couldn't recall a time that he actually hoped he wouldn't hook a fish – but that was what he hoped for as he continued fishing. Simms fished his way along the bank and inched ever closer to the first angler and was positive that wasn't their man. As he retrieved his lure and made his way around the fisherman, he paused momentarily and spoke to the elderly angler.

"Having any luck?"

"Not really. I've only been at it a short time but you know what they say, the worst day fishing is better than the best day working," said the fisherman as he let out a loud and boisterous laugh.

Unless you are being paid to fish, thought Simms. "Well, enjoy and good luck to ya."

Simms walked a bit down the shoreline and began casting again, trying to be casual and relaxed as he slowly made his way down the bank. Staying relaxed was getting a great deal harder for Simms.

About thirty yards from Simms was a man that he watched reel in and land a plump trout or salmon, he wasn't sure which. What he was certain of, however, was that the man he just watched catch that fish was the focus of his search - Johan Frank.

As Simms watched Frank bend over to retrieve his fish, Frank suddenly stopped and looked directly at Simms.

Simms thought his heart stopped. For an instant he'd locked eyes with Frank, whose stare was cold, calculating and telling of the danger that lurked within the man.

In that instant, Simms gathered every fabric of his being together and stood solid. He was staring into the eyes of a cold blooded killer. Nothing had ever prepared him for this. Could he take him out? Should he run?

As calm and steady as a skilled surgeon, Simms not only rose to the occasion – he towered over it, he owned it. Simms nodded slightly. "Hey, nice fish you have there."

In that instant it seemed as though a flood gate opened and the momentary tension between Simms and Frank was simply washed away in a torrent of apathy.

"Thanks," replied Frank as he turned his attention back to his catch.

"Look at that, would you?" said an obviously irritated DPD Officer Sharkey to his partner. "We're stuck in this car while that Simms guy is fishing. I know that's him down there talking to that old man; there's his vehicle parked right there. This sucks!"

What Sharkey didn't know was that Barry Simms thought that things were pretty crappy too, downright shitty in fact.

"Be patient dude, he's just checking out those fishermen, making sure they're not Johan Frank," said Sharkey's partner.

"Well crap, where's he going now?" Sharkey asked out loud, knowing that his partner didn't know the answer anymore than he did.

Officer Sharkey watched as Simms backtracked and slowly fished his way back to the boat ramp where he seemed to be in a conversation with a couple of guys leaning up against a boat they'd recently pulled out of the lake.

Sharkey heard the men roar with laughter and one even slapped Simms on the back which just raised his level of exasperation. "What the hell, this guy is screwing around and all I want to do is get home and eat. I'm tired and hungry. Shit!"

Sharkey watched as Simms eventually gathered his fishing gear and slowly walked to his car. Simms didn't even give them a second look as he walked past their vehicle. Simms simply started his car, backed up and drove off in the direction of Dillingham on the Lake Road.

Sharkey was livid as he turned to his partner. "What the fuck!"

Chapter 28

Blaine's phone rang and he recognized the caller I.D. number. "Hi Donny, I was hoping you'd call. The shit is hittin' the fan over here but we still have this matter of Ronald Spaulding to take care of."

Blaine Alexander filled in the King Salmon based trooper on what had transpired since they last talked. King Salmon was about seventy-five air miles from Dillingham but it was separated by Bristol Bay and as such there were no connecting roads. The news of what was happening in Dillingham hadn't reached Trooper Kramer.

Donny Kramer let out a low whistle. "I know the lieutenant is gonna be pissed he's traveling and missing out on all the fun. The rest of the Dillingham troopers are out of town too; you guys are somewhat shorthanded over there."

"Well, fortunately Jake Rohn and another investigator from his office are here and you know those two have connections as well as experience," said Blaine.

"I guess you're right. About our situation, I have orders from Anchorage. A trooper investigator and a couple of guys from the crime lab should be on their way to Dillingham. I spoke to them and gave your information as their point of contact when they arrive. Keep the scene where the body was found secured, stand down the majority of the search teams with the exception of the mountain rescue guys and the aircraft."

"You got it Donny; I'll let you know of any progress. Trooper Jarvis and I will stay at the PD until those guys arrive. Who's coming out?"

"I spoke to Jeff Fleener from the crime lab and Kenny Tracy from the trooper's criminal investigative unit," answered Donny.

"Oh yeah, I know Tracy, he came out on a homicide in Clark's Point last year. Straight up domestic violence case but I learned quite a lot from him, good man. We'll be waiting," said Blaine.

Blaine hung up with Trooper Kramer and returned to the squad room at the PD.

We all listened to the update and direction Blaine had been given about the search for Spaulding.

"Jake, Trooper Kramer had no idea about the death of Baxter or this Johan Frank person," said Blaine.

"I can't worry about the political bullshit attached to this. I let Mark Dillon know what's happening and at the present Baxter's death investigation belongs to the PD here anyway. I firmly believe I have a stake in this since someone is gunning for me, after all. I have to leave the notification dynamics and all the politics that goes along with that to Mark Dillon," I said.

Trooper Jarvis realized his face was flushed. He was there with his K-9 to help with the search for Spaulding. He knew that if Chief Perry or Rohn needed him to help in some way to catch this Johan Frank, he'd be Johnny on the spot. He was excited at the opportunity to be in on such an exciting case but knew he was too much of a rookie at this business to run such an investigation.

I got up from my chair. "Speaking of Mark Dillon, I need to touch base with him. Excuse me for a bit," I said as I walked out of the squad room and into the chief's office and closed the door behind me.

I dialed Mark's number and it seemed the call would go to his voicemail but I finally heard Mark's familiar voice answer. "I was on the other line with Julie Dancer. I guess the joke is on me. It seems the feds really do want Frank. They're being quiet about what the plan is but they've told Julie we're to stand down our pursuit of this prick and merely keep an eye out for Frank and report to them. Can you believe that?"

"That's bullshit Mark; I'm not gonna stand by while this asshole gets a pass just because the feds want to question him. He killed your friend who was protecting me! We need to hang up and you can tell Julie that you can't reach me on my cell and have left messages for me to call you. Hell, that's not hard to believe since out here the phone service is so shitty."

Mark was silent but spoke up eventually. "You have another day Jake, after that I have to officially tell you to stand down. It's going to take the feds that long to get there anyway."

I wasn't going to argue with Mark. "You got it boss."

I filled Mark in on the search and rescue and body being found.

"I guess the troopers have too much going on at the moment to worry about our problem," said Mark.

"Yeah, I don't see any connection with that situation and Baxter's death but stranger things have happened. Blaine is running things on site here for the search and we're on the same page with the two events," I added.

"Sounds good," said Mark.

I ended the call with Mark and once I hung up, I thought I should call Whitney. Shit, we were married a few days ago and now I have my neck on the line. This isn't cool at all.

"Hi Jacob, I've been worried like crazy. What's going on?" asked Whitney with her patented soothing compassion.

"I miss you Whitney. I really believe this is close to being over."

"How do you know? I mean, tell me what's been going on since you made me leave Dillingham."

Since I'd made a pact to always be straightforward with Whitney, I thought I should tell her everything. Actually she made me promise I'd always be honest with her about my work, or else! Not wanting to ever get to *'or else,'* I told her everything that had happened and naturally Whitney reacted as expected.

"A trained killer is after you Jacob! I can't take this; you can't take this. We can't take this stress!" Whitney shouted into the phone.

Not that I blamed her. She loved me but who signs up for this kind of thing?

"Whitney," I began. "You're safe. There are twenty guys here protecting me, and from what Mark just told me the feds are on their way. Everything is gonna be okay and we'll get this guy."

Man, the same speech I'd given this woman time and time again. Married barely a week and I already understood why so many cop marriages end up in the *'big D.'*

"Jacob, not to change the subject but do you remember how we talked about me selling my coffee cart business? Well, I think I want to take that last offer I got. I think it would be best if I sold the Cup-A-Joe."

How could I argue with her? Whitney started that business before I knew her. She'd paid for her education working the coffee trade. That was how we met in the first place. Her cart was near the courthouse in Anchorage and one glorious day I'd drawn the short straw and had to make the coffee run for the DA's office and the other guys waiting to testify. Well, the rest is history; Whitney was the one who helped me with that order. It was love at first sight and now we're married.

I've had this strange relationship with coffee since I first met Whitney. I didn't like the stuff but it's always been a bizarre comfort to me when I was away from Whitney. The smell of a hot cup of coffee had a way of soothing me.

"You know I support you completely."

"Are you sure Jacob? I don't have a job yet and though I plan to someday have my own business again, I believe I need some real experience to prepare me for something exciting and hopefully profitable somewhere down the road," explained Whitney.

I think she was trying to convince herself or perhaps trying to take her mind off of what was happening in Dillingham.

"Does this mean I can stop pretending to like coffee?"

Chapter 29

I had no sooner disconnected my call with Whitney than my cell phone buzzed again. It was Barry Simms.

It was about time that Simms called to check-in. It was getting late and I wanted to know that they were all okay first of all and secondly I'd hoped to have positive news concerning the search for Frank. "Barry, talk to me."

"We have him; well not *'have'* actually, but I spotted Frank!" blurted out an excited Barry.

"Where? Do you still have him under surveillance?" I opened the door to the chief's office and called for him to join me.

"At the lake, but I've lost sight of him," said Barry.

"Blaine and Trooper Jarvis went to the airport," announced the chief as he entered his office.

I set my phone down on the desk and pressed the speaker button. "Barry, I have the chief with me, now explain what you were just telling me."

"Well," began Barry. "I spotted Frank at Aleknagik Lake. Scared the shit out of me! I was close enough to him that I could practically smell his body odor. He was fishing, do you believe that? He was fishing like a damn tourist on vacation. He saw me looking at him but I think we're good; he didn't make me. I was sorta caught by surprise; there were other people around us, so I backed away. I saw the two PD guys in the parking lot but ignored them and got in my car and drove up the Lake Road. I pulled off into the trees but was able to watch the road and any cars that would pass by. I managed to flag down Sharkey and his partner as they followed along after me."

"So where's Frank now?" I asked.

"He left the lake just a few minutes ago and is alone heading toward Dillingham. He's in an old blue Dodge pickup; Sharkey said that the old truck Frank was driving belongs to Barney Shear who works cargo for one of the airlines at the airport," explained Barry.

"Barry, do you have anything more to add?" I asked.

"No, that's it. It took us a few minutes to get where I had a cell signal but I called you right away," said Barry.

"Okay, give Frank about a ten minute head start and then slowly drive back to Dillingham. Have Sharkey and his partner follow you. Maybe you can spot Frank if he turns off the road, but don't confront him," I instructed Barry.

"Okay, got it," said Barry before he disconnected the call.

"Chief, call all your men and let them know what we're looking for and have them see if they can spot Frank as he gets close to town. I'll call Blaine and give him a heads up too. If he's picking up those guys from Anchorage they'll be headed to Aleknagik in order to get to that body they discovered. We don't want anyone to be surprised," I said.

"No problem, I'll get on it. I know Barney Shear and I know that pickup. I think we need to go pay Barney a visit," added Chief Perry.

I nodded. "Good idea."

I called Blaine Alexander. He and Trooper Jarvis had met the trooper investigator and the crime lab techs. It turned out to be Jeff Fleener and Carlos who'd been sent out to Dillingham once again. They'd returned to Anchorage the day before after spending half a day collecting evidence from Baxter's crime scene and also near Blaine's home where we believed Frank had stood for a time while staking out Blaine's house.

The trooper investigator, Kenny Tracy, apparently was all kinds of wrapped around the axle; no one had taken the time to explain to him a killer was on the loose in Dillingham, a dangerous man the feds were after. The entire time that I spoke with Blaine on the phone I could hear Tracy spewing profanities in the background. Saying he was pissed off was an understatement.

Tracy had been told he was going out to investigate the death of a missing hiker or fisherman and even the circumstances around that wasn't clear to him. Blaine had at least been able to explain both the Johan Frank business and the odd circumstances of finding a buried body while searching for the overdue fisherman. Blaine had a way of coming across so non-confrontational. I felt he could connect with anyone he took a notion to. Another reason I thought Blaine could go far in this business.

The chief returned to the squad room after I'd completed my call to Blaine. "Okay, I talked to my patrols. I passed along the information about Shear's old pickup and they were familiar with it. The unmarked units are on their way to the Lake Road where they hope to spot Frank or the vehicle he'd been seen driving."

"Great, you ready to go see Shear?" I asked.

As we drove to Shear's house on the edge of town, Chief Perry told me that the two plainclothes patrols had checked with the different hotels in town and didn't have any luck finding anyone who'd seen Frank or recognized him as having checked into their respective locations.

As we pulled up to Shear's house it looked like most of the local residences in the area to some degree. A boat, or skiff, was on a trailer parked near the wood framed home. There were two dogs tethered to the front part of the structure. A working, and likely a non-working, snowmachine were up on blocks, awaiting the snowfall that residents weren't expecting for a few more months. Smoke was trailing upward from an aluminum smoke stack on the roof and a wood pile dominated one side of the house.

As we approached the home of Barney Shear, Chief Perry pointed out that the vehicle parked there also belonged to Shear. The old Dodge pickup was nowhere to be seen.

A balding man with a round belly opened the door once the chief knocked.

"Hi Barney," began the chief. "Sorry to bug you but we have a few questions."

"Who's this with you?" asked Barney while gesturing toward me.

"Allow me to introduce Jake Rohn, an investigator from Anchorage; this is about a case we both are working on," explained the chief.

"What case?" asked Barney while cautiously eyeing me.

I produced my credentials and showed them to Barney. That seemingly appeased him because he stopped staring at me as if I had a horn protruding from my forehead.

The chief laughed quietly. "Come on Barney, you know how this works; we ask the questions when we're questioning you."

Barney finally relaxed. His momentary wariness was replaced with a smile while he chuckled. "How can I help you two?"

"It's about your old Dodge pickup; where is it?" the chief asked directly.

"Oh, is that all? I don't know. I sold it to some guy a few days back. He gave me five grand for a pickup that wasn't worth anywhere near that much," answered Barney.

I spoke up, "Isn't that sorta strange?"

"Not to me," Barney replied. "I rent or sell that old pickup four or five times a summer. There are very few rental cars here in Dillingham. I work out at the airport and when people don't think ahead and then want a vehicle to rent while they're here they ask around and I've let it be known I have a pickup that can be rented, or bought even. Word gets around and they get sent my way. The couple of times it's been bought, they always bring it back and I take it off their hands quite a bit cheaper than what it originally sold for. I suspect it will come back again this time too. Why are you asking about my old Dodge?"

"Barney, that's price gouging," said the chief.

"I completely disagree, chief," said Barney. "It's all about supply and demand," Barney grinned.

I produced a close-up photo of Frank and showed it to Barney. "Is this the guy who bought your pickup?"

Barney answered without hesitation. "Sure is!"

"Did he say why he needed the pickup or for how long?" asked the chief.

Barney rubbed the stubble on his chin. I thought how much he reminded me of Fred Flintstone which I thought was funny since his name was Barney.

"He just said he made last minute plans to get out here for some fishing and hunting and needed a vehicle. He said he'd heard I owned a pickup I would sell to him but he didn't say how long he was going to be here. I've heard that same story several times before. This isn't L.A., we don't have a bunch of cars sittin' around just waiting to be rented," Barney laughed again.

Chief Perry seemed satisfied with Barney's explanation. "Jake, do you have any other questions for Barney?"

I shook my head from side to side. "No, but Barney, I need two things from you and maybe I'll forget about the price gouging thing."

Barney looked as though I had his attention now. All the wittiness had left his responses and the color drained from his face which is what I intended. He didn't need to know I had no idea if there was a price gouging law in Alaska and if there was, I could give a shit less at the moment.

"Sure, whatever you need," said a now attentive Barney.

"One," I began. "Don't breathe a single word of this conversation or our visit to anyone."

"Forgotten; no problem," said Barney.

"Two," I continued. "If you see this guy again, act as if nothing has happened and as soon as you get a chance, you call Chief Perry."

"No problem there either," Barney said quite convincingly.

After the chief and I left Barney I couldn't help but laugh.

"Chief, Barney's a good man...It's in his best interest and safety if Frank doesn't even think there's a chance the cops questioned him. Frank would kill him in an instant if he thought there was the slightest possibility we were on to him."

"Yeah, I understand," said the chief. "Barney is normally a smart ass, you had his asshole puckered up, and I thought I was gonna burst out laughing. Price gouging . . . Damn! That was some funny shit."

Chapter 30

It was getting late. This had been a long day, longer than any day had been for quite some time. The chief was finishing up talking with his dispatcher and calling all of his patrol units by phone.

I had a message on my cell phone from Blaine Alexander. They'd reached Aleknagik Lake. He was taking the troopers and crime lab techs up to the end of the lake where the body had been found. There was a state owned cabin available fairly close that was vacant and large enough for all of them to crash for the night. He'd be able to reach the search team securing the body and the search base by VHF radio once they arrived at their destination. Most importantly, Blaine related to me that they didn't see that old blue pickup of Barney Shear's.

I also spoke with Barry Simms; just like Blaine, he hadn't located or found any evidence of the old blue Dodge pickup or Johan Frank. It was as if Frank had disappeared. The Lake Road possessed a few pullouts and a couple of other roads that branched off from it that eventually turned into trails but that was about it until you reached Dillingham. Frank may be staying in the old truck or even camped up a trail or something similar. There was quite a lot of ground to cover and it was rather late and almost completely dark. Not conducive to favorable search conditions, especially when the search was for the likes of Johan Frank.

They needed to make a plan – the feds were going to show up the following day and once they did that, there was no telling what would happen. I knew that I most certainly wouldn't like the outcome unless it included putting a bullet in Frank's head. That man wouldn't be taken alive. I was sure of that.

Barry Simms was going to call it a day. I thought I should do the same. There was a bunk with my name on it and I really needed the rest.

Chief Perry entered his office and dropped heavily into his chair. He kicked back and put his feet up on his desk. "Well, I talked with everyone I have out there. No one has seen that damn old pickup Frank was driving. I sent everyone home except one set of uniformed guys. They'll be staying at the station pretty much all night unless called out. I have worn out all of my resources."

I stifled a yawn. "I understand chief, this is hard on everyone. I got a message from Blaine and spoke to Barry Simms. They didn't see anything. Blaine and that crew are out of the picture for now. Simms is staying at the same B&B where Baxter had been killed."

Chief Perry stood and stretched. "Let's call it a night and get back to it bright and early tomorrow. The rest will be good for us both."

I thought there was something more we could or should be doing but I knew that the chief was right; we all needed some rest. "Okay, I'm staying right here in your transient quarters if you need me. I promise not to leave the building without you or one of your officers being with me. How about we meet here at six or seven; you can buy me breakfast."

"Good enough; I'll see you in the morning."

Chuck Jones was roughing it for the fourth night in a row. He needed a bath and a hot meal; not only hot food but real food would be ideal. He sat alone, on a log he'd pulled up close to the fire.

The last two nights he elected to have a small fire, but even that wasn't making him comfortable any longer. He felt at ease with having a fire and didn't believe he was taking a risk. His makeshift camp was far enough away from the road that the flames from the tiny fire were basically impossible to be seen by anyone who may be driving by during the night. Jones didn't want to draw any attention to his camp.

Tomorrow was the day Rohn and his bride should return from their trip. With the fishing he'd done at the lake, he was actually jealous that Rohn was most likely getting in some fantastic fishing in addition to the joys of being newly married. If he hadn't been hired to kill Rohn he'd want to befriend the man and the two of them could go out together and slay some trophy fish.

He'd made several checks around town where he believed Rohn would most likely be, but so far he hadn't found anything that would lead him to believe Rohn had returned to Dillingham. He had to be careful; Dillingham was small and it was best for him to tread lightly.

The decision had already been made; the following day he planned to stake out Shannon's pond and watch the air taxi that flew Rohn out to the remote cabin. When Rohn returned he'd snipe him from the cover of the trees and make his getaway, catch a plane and get the hell out of town. He'd already scoped out his sniper position as well as his getaway route. There were five different flights to Anchorage from Dillingham starting at about noon. He had reservations on all of those flights – each under a different name.

If things didn't turn out as he hoped, he still planned to leave town. He should have waited for Rohn to return to Anchorage to begin with. He was unable to shake the feeling that traveling to Dillingham was a mistake. What was the big hurry after all? He underestimated the difficulty he would have in completing this contract in anonymity, in such a small community. He hated to admit to himself but he was wrong in the way he approached and rushed this job.

It was settled; this comes to an end tomorrow or it would have to wait until Rohn returned to Anchorage. He'd taken far too many chances and was making rookie mistakes such as killing Baxter, having Baxter's phone go off while he was in that store and that angler staring at him for several seconds as he caught that fish earlier in the day. All examples of drawing attention to himself, attention he didn't want or need. He survived for twenty years in this business by not making such errors. Good thing he was in a little backwater town and they weren't on to him but his luck can't last. He leaves tomorrow, job finished or not.

Jones stirred and fed the small fire and then stared into the flames. Usually when he had a lot of down time like this he reflected on who he was, where he came from and how he got to be the man he was today. Born to German parents who lived in New York, he spent the first part of his life as Johan Frank. He couldn't recall the last time he'd been called his given name.

When recruited by the American government to do their bidding, their dirty work, his head was filled with so many lies and false expectations. *'It's their fault he's the dangerous man that he had become,'* he thought.

He was bitter; the sad thing was he couldn't be sure who he hated the most. Was it the ones responsible for turning him into the monster he was? Or was it himself?

He was taught how to kill, how to survive, and how to be anybody he needed to be in order to endure and persevere. The ones who were in charge of his training would love to get their hands on him, extract whatever information they could and then kill him. He'd never be taken alive, that was another decision that was already made.

It was time to get some rest; the coming day would be long and tedious. He intended to be up early and had decided to have breakfast in town by six in the morning, before most people even got out of bed. He looked forward to a hot meal, a real meal. He damn sure deserved it.

Chapter 31

I tossed and turned the entire night. It's essential that we find this Johan Frank bastard before he finds me. I believed today would be our last chance to locate him in Dillingham. The feds will shut us down once they arrived, and hell, even if we found Frank and are able to capture him alive, the feds would just take him anyway.

Somewhat of a no win scenario for us. We kill him, he kills me or the feds take him and of course there's the possibility he could get away completely. With us knowing what he looks like it will be much more difficult for him to get on a plane. TSA had been alerted and provided information about Frank and they're already on the lookout for him. I guess he could charter a plane or hitch a ride on one of the commercial fishing vessels that are based somewhere other than Dillingham.

I certainly didn't like the idea that Frank could make a clean get away. I also wasn't thrilled with the thought of looking over my shoulder wondering where he was or when he'd show up. If this Marcus has me in his crosshairs for that mess up in Fort Yukon, he's one vindictive asshole and won't stop until I'm dead and gone.

Mark Dillon had asked me on my wedding day if there was some other connection I may have to Marcus other than that case up north. If he only knew how much time and effort I've put into trying to figure that out! I just can't make a connection or recall anything that I did in Colorado that would answer that question.

The one thing that bothered me the most was the nagging question as to why some professional killer, with the apparent training, expertise and experience that Johan Frank was reported to have, was lollygagging around Aleknagik Lake? Why isn't he laying in wait for me somewhere?

If it had been possible, a thought bubble with a bright light inside it would have appeared over my head, just as in a cartoon when one of the characters is struck with a great idea.

He was waiting for me! Frank knew where I went after I arrived in Dillingham. Whitney and I traveled to a remote lake and cabin, and were due to come back today. Frank found out we'd left town and has been waiting for me to return; he somehow figured out our schedule. Apparently he hasn't learned we came back earlier than planned. That has to be it; he had to have known!

I was up and ready for the chief to arrive at the PD by 6:30 a.m. I simply puttered about while I waited for the chief to get in. It may have been a bit of a long shot but I had an idea how to find out what Frank may have known about my travels. While I sat deep in thought the chief entered the squad room where I had elected to kill some time.

"Good morning sunshine, how'd ya sleep?" asked the chief.

"Not worth a damn. I believe I would've accomplished more if I'd stayed awake all night worrying about everything."

"I ordered us breakfast. The restaurant here doesn't normally deliver but it's sometimes good to know the staff there; it didn't take much to convince them to deliver our order," gloated the chief.

"I'm starving, thanks."

"You said last night that I was buying. Since I was too tired to argue about it this morning I just thought it was easier to let you have your way," the chief said laughingly.

Honestly, it always seemed that when you put two cops together, they were constantly squabbling over who was buying the current meal. The funny thing though is that in the long run, it always evened out.

"Well, thanks again. To move on, I did have a thought about what Frank was up to. It's been really eating at me as to why he's off fishing and not looking for me or waiting to ambush me somewhere. I mean hell; he's acting like a tourist."

The chief nodded. "You know, I was thinking the same thing."

"So, if he's as good as we have been told, I think he's been waiting for me, waiting for me to get back to town which was supposed to be today."

I could tell the wheels were in motion now; the chief had this far away look in his eyes. He almost immediately returned from the internal searching process and his eyes again focused on me. "He had to have known; someone told him you and Whitney had flown out of town for a few days."

"Chief, that's exactly what I'm thinking. So far we can pretty much assume he doesn't know I'm back. Why else would he be so carefree in a sense, as if he was on a break."

"Who knew you were in town and what your plans were?"

I thought about that for a few seconds. "That's a short list; my boss, Whitney of course, Baxter, Blaine Alexander and his wife. That was basically it; a few others such as friends and family in Anchorage, but all they knew was that we were coming out here after our wedding, not the details of what we were planning. Frank obviously knew we were travelling to Dillingham since he followed us or maybe even arrived before we did."

There was a definite pause as Chief Perry absorbed what I'd said.

I continued my thought. "None of them would have had a reason to tell anyone but I can call Blaine's wife and ask her if anyone came around asking questions.

I seriously doubt Baxter had the opportunity to say anything and from what I've learned about the man he wouldn't talk anyway. If Frank had tried to get information out of Baxter, I suspect that crime scene would have been completely different. There would have been a significant struggle," said the chief.

As the chief spoke it became clear; I knew the answer. "Our air charter, that has to be the link. They knew exactly what my schedule was. They flew us out to the lake and knew when to come and pick us up. I doubt they would blatantly advertise what their client's schedules were but if someone asked the right questions they very likely could learn quite a lot of information."

"You could be right about that, now that you mention it. There are just three charter services at Shannon's pond and I know all the employees. It will be a bit over an hour before they open but I can contact them and see if they've seen anyone hanging around out there and maybe asking some pointed questions."

"Okay chief, sounds good. I'm gonna call Barry Simms and get him over here so that we can touch base about what he's done and to formulate a plan. Maybe our food will arrive soon. I'm still starving."

The chief stood to return to his office. "Any word on Barney's old pickup?"

"Nothing, I doubt Barry has anything to report. He would've already told us if he did."

Not long after, our food arrived. We ate the hardy and filling meal pretty much in silence. The chief ordered enough food for ten people; he must have woken up hungry. Barry Simms arrived and had some of our breakfast as there was plenty. We finished eating and since it was almost 8:30 the chief went to his office to begin making calls to the air charters at Shannon's pond. We thought it best if we stayed at the office rather than drive out to Shannon's pond and perhaps be seen by Frank. That could ruin any chance of locating him, or worse.

I sent Barry Simms back to Aleknagik Lake in hopes he could spot Frank. We elected to utilize two regular marked patrols in Dillingham to hopefully locate the pickup Frank was seen driving. If my theory was correct, Frank will be in Dillingham waiting for me, not off fishing at the lake.

I dialed Mark Dillon's cell phone and he answered on the first ring. "Hi Jake, any news?"

"Well, Frank was spotted at the lake late yesterday. He was fishing, for heaven's sake. Frank got mobile and disappeared before any plan could be made to try and take him down."

I took Mark's silence for the pause needed for his brain to formulate the first of at least a hundred questions. Finally he spoke.

"Do you know where he is?"

"No. We believe he's somewhere between Dillingham and Aleknagik but can't be certain. We know what he's driving but can't find his vehicle either. He's not at any hotel or B&B. I suspect he's been hiding out in the woods where he can't be easily spotted," I answered, in hopes to take a few of Mark's questions out of play.

Mark paused again. I figured I'd done a good enough job of covering at least the essential questions.

"I just got off the phone with Julie. She's fairly slow on the uptake of things but she was able to relate to me that you can expect the feds out there early this afternoon."

I laughed. "Okay, so that means sometime between tonight and next Friday considering the feds normal timeline."

"Really funny Jake. You just keep your ass from getting shot off and don't do anything that will jeopardize anyone else's safety."

I tried to be serious. Mark made me laugh with the mental image of all of us standing around looking down at my ass lying on the ground and wondering how I would explain to Mark how I let it get shot off. "You got it Mark; I'll let you know if there's any news."

Johan Frank saw to it that he was as comfortable as possible. He was all set for that charter to return with Rohn and he'd finish the deal and calmly leave this town before anyone had a chance to even figure out what had taken place.

He wished he hadn't downed so much coffee with his breakfast. He didn't want to move about anymore than was absolutely necessary. Though he felt his cover was almost perfect, the last thing he wanted to do was get up from his position and chance being discovered. It wouldn't be the first time he relieved himself in an awkward manner and likely wouldn't be his last.

That's why he'd been so successful in this business. He possessed the patience needed to wait out melting ice in the winter. Today would be no different. He could almost taste those tropical rum drinks with the little umbrellas in them.

He'd seen the floatplane taxi and take off about twenty minutes earlier. He suspected that Rohn would be among the passengers who would return on that very aircraft. His getaway vehicle was stashed and ready to take him to the airport once he fired the lethal shot.

The long and very familiar wait had begun.

Chapter 32

"We're in luck," announced the chief as he strolled through the door and entered the squad room.

"How's that?" I asked.

"I just got off the phone with Bella at the air taxi that took you and Whitney out to Forty Minute Lake. She remembered a phone call she received the very day their pilot flew you and Whitney out there. A prospective client called in and asked about a charter to take him to a remote fishing site. She said the caller was pleasant enough but some things stood out to her concerning the conversation."

The chief pulled out a chair at the desk next to where I was seated and sat down before continuing.

"The guy, the caller was a male by the way, didn't ask about the prices of their charters and though she thought he'd called on behalf of a group, he always referred to 'I' throughout the conversation. The thing that stood out the most was that she mentioned flying a newlywed couple out to a remote cabin on a lake and he asked what lake and if she knew when the couple would be returning so that he could check on that location and perhaps go there. She was certain she mentioned when you and Whitney were scheduled to return to Dillingham. At the time she believed the caller was interested in renting the cabin at 40 Minute Lake."

The chief had every ounce of my attention now. "Okay, is that it?" I asked.

"Well, the strange part she thought was how the man abruptly ended the call at that point and she has never heard back from him. She hasn't thought much about it but when I asked her, she immediately recalled the conversation and now felt as if the man was pumping her for information more than trying to set up a charter."

I sat back in my chair and thought about this. If this Frank joker had been watching me, he would have followed us to Shannon's Pond and knew what service we used. He made a call and learned we were due back today and has been more or less killing time until we returned. It all makes sense.

I leaned forward again. "Did you learn anything else?"

"No, I spoke to office staff of the other air charter services and even called a few residents who live along the road that leads to the airstrip and float pond. No one has seen or heard anything out of the ordinary. What Bella told me is all that anyone could recall," explained the chief.

"Chief, could this be so simple? This guy is more dangerous and certainly more criminally sophisticated than anyone either of has ever dealt with. I mean, do you think it's possible he could be watching Shannon's Pond this very minute, waiting for me to get out of a plane?"

Chief Perry looked directly at me and was quiet; he quickly gathered his thoughts and began to speak. "It seems to me that Frank feels fairly comfortable in what he's doing. I really believe he feels like his presence here has gone completely unnoticed."

I nodded in agreement. "Okay, I can see that."

The chief continued. "People think it's easy to hide out in a small town but in reality it's harder. You almost ran into him at the store and he was leisurely fishing up at the lake where Simms spotted him. Baxter's death has been kept pretty quiet. The fact that Baxter wasn't from here has made it easier to keep under wraps as well as it has been. The bulk of the talk around town has been about the search for the lost fisherman up on the Agulowak. To answer your question, yes, I believe it's entirely possible that Frank could have Shannon's Pond staked out and awaiting your return."

A cold chill ran up my spine. Just a few days ago Whitney and I were married and I was on top of the world. Then this shit starts up with that bullet from Marcus, a damn bullet with my name on it. Mark enlists his ex-fed buddy to help watch my back and he gets killed for his effort. Now there's this maniac with the skills to kill at the drop of a hat somewhere out there, gunning for me and is willing to take anyone out who stands in his way. It's his business, his life.

I guess the chief could sense or even see the distress on my face.

"Look Jake, none of this is your fault. You, like the rest of us, just want to get this guy. It's what we signed up for and we all know how it sometimes ends in tragedy. Baxter knew that too. Stop blaming yourself."

I looked up at the chief. "You're right. We need to concentrate on getting this guy before someone else dies."

About that moment, a familiar figure came through the squad room door.

"Hi Blaine," I said as he made his way over to us.

Blaine dragged up a chair and sat down. "What's going on Jake, did you find Frank?"

"Not yet. Why are you in town? Did you find your fisherman?" I asked.

"Well, I left the troopers and crime scene techs up where the body was found. They are busy working on the scene and recovering the body. I don't expect to see them until later this afternoon. I checked on the progress of the search and though we have scaled back the overall effort, there are some locals who know the area the best and those search teams from the mountain rescue group who are revisiting some of the earlier search areas just to be certain that nothing was missed," said Blaine.

Blaine was worn out from the long days of searching for Spaulding but it was clear that he was interested in learning more about Johan Frank.

"Did you see Barry Simms at the lake?" I asked Blaine.

"Yes I did; he met me at the boat launch and we spoke briefly. He told me that everyone was still looking for Barney's old pickup and Johan Frank along with it."

The chief had been quiet but interjected with a question. "On your trip back to town, any chance you saw that pickup?"

"I kept an eye out for it but haven't seen it," said Blaine.

I took a few minutes and explained to Blaine what the chief learned from speaking with Bella at Shannon's Pond.

Blaine nodded in the affirmative. "I agree, I think he could be looking for you at Shannon's Pond, or my house."

The chief and I looked at one another. We hadn't considered that possibility.

Blaine spoke up. I think he realized what he'd said caught us by surprise. "I have to stop by the trooper office; I think the lieutenant is due back today. If I can't see him I'll need to call Trooper Kramer in King Salmon and brief him on where the search for Spaulding stands. Then I'll head home where I need to get some much needed rest. I'll look my place over really well and let you know if I find anything."

"Thanks Blaine. I know your wife is still at her mom's house but you let me know when you get home," I said.

Blaine stood and moved toward the door. "Okay Jake, will do. I'll see you guys later."

After Blaine had left us the chief spoke up. "What's the plan Jake?"

"How about we get two of your guys to go undercover? They can dress to blend in with the locals and have them maybe deliver some packages or something out to Shannon's Pond and up the Lake Road. With any luck they may spot Barney's old pickup or something else that will help us out."

"That'll work. I can get one of the freight vans from the airport and put two of my guys in it. They can drive all around out there and occasionally make stops or whatever, all the while really scouring the entire area. Finding Barney's old pickup could be the key; that's Frank's only transportation it would seem."

My phone buzzed and I saw that I had received a text message from Blaine. He was notifying me that all was clear around his home. I answered him back and told him thanks for letting me know.

About that moment my cell phone rang; it was Barry Simms.

"Hi Barry, how's it going out there?"

"There's nothing happening at all here at the lake. What do you want me to do?"

I took a couple of minutes and explained to Barry the lead regarding Shannon's Pond and how we intended to make the effort to find Barney's old pickup if not Johan Frank himself. I also let him in on what Mark passed along concerning the feds' arrival, that they were expected to be in Dillingham later that day and we'd likely be taking orders from them or told to get out of their way completely.

"I think it's best if you just stay there for now. I'll let you know what we find, if anything."

"Alright Jake. If you can't reach me on my phone, leave a message. I'll get back to you as soon as I can," said Barry.

After I was finished speaking to Barry, the chief returned to the squad room.

"Alright Jake, I have my two guys lined out and they are on their way to pick up a vehicle right now. They have instructions to find that old pickup of Barney's and let us know right away."

"I guess we sit back and be patient. Waiting is the hardest part in my opinion," I said as I leaned back in my chair and settled in for a long and anxious delay.

Chapter 33

It had been perhaps an hour since the chief had left me alone in the squad room. I was getting quite nervous, so I went and chatted with the dispatcher for a few minutes. I had no sooner returned to the squad room and sat down than Chief Perry came into the room and began talking excitedly.

"We found him!"

"Frank, you found Frank?" I repeated.

"Well, not him exactly but my guys found his vehicle."

I could feel the excitement, adrenaline and importance of the moment overtaking me. "Where?"

Chief Perry moved close to a large map on the wall. "Come over here and I'll show you."

I got up and crossed the room and stood near the chief as he pointed at the map.

"This is where the Lake Road begins and leads out of Dillingham. A couple of miles down the Lake Road is the turnoff that takes you to Shannon's Pond. There's just the one road in and one road out of Shannon's Pond. About a quarter mile past that turnoff is one of those telephone utility buildings that's maybe fifty yards off the Lake Road. Behind that utility building is where my men found the old Dodge pickup that Frank was driving, parked in the edge of the trees."

I looked at the map and had a good idea of the area the chief was describing as I had been to Shannon's Pond and had driven the Lake Road.

"Any sign of Frank?" I asked.

"No, they had turned down the driveway that goes to the building and when they spotted the vehicle, they backed up and pulled out onto the Lake Road. They drove down about a hundred yards and are parked in the driveway of a private residence where they are able see the utility building driveway and are watching to ensure Frank doesn't drive off and we lose him again. The access they are watching is the only way to get onto the Lake Road from the utility building," explained the chief.

"Okay I get it. So from the Lake Road to Shannon's Pond it's almost a mile. I doubt Frank was staying that close to town for fear of being spotted so he has to be staking out the float pond and air taxi in hopes of spotting me," I said.

"We need to figure out how to approach this so that we can apprehend Frank before he does get away for good," said Chief Perry.

"I have an idea chief; we can use that vehicle as bait and make a plan to get Frank when he comes back to get it. Let me make some calls and then we can get things rolling before we miss our chance."

I called Barry Simms and told him to return to the PD and meet with us. We had located Frank's vehicle and wanted to make a plan about how we could apprehend the fugitive when he returned to it, if he actually does return to it. Either way, we felt this was our best and only opportunity to put an end to this. I also called Blaine Alexander but all I reached was his voicemail, so I left a message. My last call was to Mark Dillon. I explained to Mark what we had discovered and he told me to do what was necessary in order to apprehend Frank. We didn't want to take a chance of anyone else getting hurt.

I hung up with Mark and turned to the chief. "I'm ready to get at this. Mark had not heard anything more definite from the feds and we have no idea where they are, so this is still our show."

While I was on the phone with Mark, Chief Perry had called the trooper office and spoke with Lieutenant Rivers who had in fact returned to Dillingham that morning. Lieutenant Rivers was excited to get in on the capture of Frank and was on his way to the PD.

Chief Perry and I began making plans and when Lieutenant Rivers arrived we filled him in on everything that had happened while he was out of town.

I used a hand drawn map of where the vehicle was located to illustrate the plan. "There will be six of us in all. Let's split off into teams of three. Myself, Barry and the lieutenant will be one team. Chief, you and your two guys will be the other."

I drew in a location for each of the teams on the map. "One team will be hidden in the trees to the front of the vehicle and the other team will be on the driver's side of the vehicle in the brush near the building. This will form an 'L' to prevent a crossfire situation if it comes to that."

Lieutenant Rivers spoke up. "I suggest we disable the vehicle if possible and at least situate a spike strip across the access road just in case. I have one in my vehicle we can use."

I nodded. "Good idea. We all need to wear camouflage and go as far as covering our heads, hands and face. We must get as close to Frank's vehicle as possible to be able to control him at the perfect moment but far enough away in order to remain undetected."

"There is plenty of gear for us all right here at the PD. We've been collecting old military BDUs for quite some time," added Chief Perry.

I continued with the plan. "What do you say if we have all team members armed with handguns and two with pepper ball guns, two with shotguns and two with rifles?"

Both Chief Perry and Lieutenant Rivers agreed.

"This can turn out to be a long wait, if Frank is waiting on me and I don't show. There's no telling how long he will stay in place before he gives up for the day. I think we need to be prepared to stay until dark and perhaps at that point back off. I'm sure the feds will be here by then anyway and undoubtedly will have their own plan," I said.

Lieutenant Rivers stood up. "Sounds good. I'll meet you back here in twenty minutes with gear and food. I can pick up enough for us all to have something to eat and drink. This may end up being a long wait as you said."

"I agree," said the chief. "I'll get our gear together and be here waiting."

As I was getting my own gear together at the PD, Barry Simms showed up. I explained to him the basics of the plan we had formulated and then I helped him get together what he needed in the way of camouflage clothing and a shotgun from the PD.

I was going to be equipped with a rifle and Lieutenant Rivers would be equipped with a pepper ball gun in my group. I knew that Chief Perry was going to carry a shotgun; he said his eyes weren't what they used to be and he preferred a shotgun over a rifle. There would be a rifle and pepper ball gun in the chief's group as well.

It was thirty minutes later that we all left the PD. We were eager to get in place and begin our wait for Frank. Chief Perry had been in constant contact with his men who were watching Frank's vehicle and there had been no change. It was 12:30 p.m. I hoped and prayed that we hadn't missed the opportunity to catch Baxter's killer.

Chapter 34

Johan Frank had been lying in his place of concealment for several hours now. His view of the pond where the floatplanes took off and landed was unobstructed. He determined the distance with his rangefinder to be precisely two-hundred yards to the water's edge from his vantage point. The place he had chosen was where he needed to be in order to get the job accomplished.

Frank had sipped on water and chewed beef jerky to keep his body fueled and ready for action. He was beginning to wonder if Rohn had changed plans or had returned to Dillingham early. He felt as though he could kick himself in the ass for not approaching this job with his usual meticulous demeanor. He had no idea why he was drifting; he was unable to give his full attention to his work. Now, he was more certain than ever that he was doing his final job. He couldn't help but think of the good life he would have once he returned home and set his retirement plan into action. Sun and surf were definitely in his future. He had been with women but had never been in a lasting or meaningful relationship; perhaps it was time for that as well.

He had watched the two separate aircraft from Rohn's air taxi come and go once apiece. Rohn wasn't a passenger on any of the return flights. It was approaching 1:00 in the afternoon but there was plenty of time left for his target to return to Dillingham before he would consider calling it a day. He needed to exercise more patience. He has waited much longer than this for a mark to find their way into the crosshairs of the scope on his Parker-Hale M-85 7.62 MM sniper rifle. There was no reason to panic just yet. Even so, the plan was to return to Anchorage today even if he missed the opportunity to get Rohn.

His plan was simple. Wait for Rohn to deplane and once he was in the clear, he intended on putting a bullet through Rohn's head which would cause it to explode, resulting in instantaneous death. He would be able to make the three-quarters of a mile jog back to his vehicle in ten minutes or so and be long gone before anyone begins to figure out what had even happened, much less where the shot had come from. Piece of cake. They weren't ready for his kind in Dillingham. He didn't need to give this job his full attention all the time. He could practically do this in his sleep.

Frank could feel the confidence in himself returning. It was a warm feeling engulfing his body as if he was sunbathing on a hot beach. The warmth spread to his limbs and permeated his mind. Yeah, this would be easy enough to finish; no worries here.

We decided to meet up at a house that was about a quarter mile away and across the Lake Road from where Frank's vehicle was located. Chief Perry had notified the fire chief who contacted four of his medics to meet us there with an ambulance. The chief knew the area well and chose a perfect staging area to conceal us from Frank if he was already returning to his vehicle.

Barry Simms and Lieutenant Rivers relieved the two PD officers who were watching out for Frank's vehicle so that they could gear up and get the details of what we planned to do.

Everyone gathered around me as I spread out the map on the hood of my vehicle and again outlined our operation. "Each of you should make sure your phones are off, radios are off and you have everything you need, once we are in place that's where we will stay until either Frank shows up or I give the fall back signal. Any questions?"

I looked around at the men who were intently staring at me. Chief Perry was hardened by time and experience. I knew he would be fine. His two young officers were nervous. I had no reason to believe that they would be a burden or unable to react but thought they needed to have more of a pep talk to help them get their minds right.

I recalled what a patrol sergeant once told me in Colorado Springs when I was a rookie cop. His words had stayed with me for years and I took part of what he told me and passed it on to my group. "This Johan Frank is very likely the most dangerous man any of us will come across in our lifetimes. We know this, but we also know he's just a man. We all are nervous; we all are perhaps even a little scared. That's okay; those feelings are natural and good to have but we can't let them control us. Having none of those feelings would be a reason to be worried. Remember our plan; know you have all of us there to back you up."

Chief Perry slapped me on the back. "Are you ready for this Jake?" I was certainly feeling the adrenaline flowing myself. Adrenaline made it impossible for me to distinguish nerves from fear.

I nodded in the affirmative and we hit the trail along the Lake Road and within minutes we were alongside Barry Simms and Lieutenant Rivers.

I crouched near Barry. "You guys see anything?"

"Nothing," said Barry.

I turned and faced the group. "Last minute gear check guys, make sure everything is ready before we go."

Everyone quickly checked all their gear and weapons and made sure their phones and radios were indeed off. Just a few moments after 1:00 p.m. our six man team headed out in single file. We crossed the Lake Road and made our way to the access that led to the utility building. Lieutenant Rivers quickly deployed a spike strip across the narrow road and then we continued to the utility building itself.

Within a minute, Chief Perry and his two men were situated among the trees in some low brush about sixty feet directly in front of Frank's vehicle. Their cover was working perfectly; I could only locate them because I knew where they were and I had the luxury of being able to stare until I actually could see an outline of an arm or another body part. They were hidden very well for the hurried approach we were forced to take.

Frank's vehicle was parked behind the utility building and was parallel to the Lake Road. That put the vehicle between the building and Shannon's Pond. Chief Perry and his men were facing the front of the vehicle and we suspected Frank would be coming from the direction of Shannon's Pond or from the chief's left.

Me and Lieutenant Rivers were facing the driver side of Frank's vehicle and were adjacent to the utility building about forty-five feet from the driver's door. Barry Simms was on the other end of the utility building and facing the driver's side as well. I thought we had very good cover in the low brush and willows that were growing around the building. We were facing the direction of Shannon's Pond and the chief was to our left.

Lieutenant Rivers and Barry Simms approached the driver side of the vehicle before they took cover. They tried the door and it was unlocked. Barry slid into the vehicle and locked the passenger door and driver door before softly closing it. We thought that was the best thing to do rather than trying to disable the vehicle which might take more time and run the risk of making noises that may alert Frank to our presence.

Once in place, the warmth of the day began getting to us all. We were heavily clothed in long sleeves with our hands, heads and faces covered with cloth or camouflage paint, the cream kind you see hunters apply to their skin. The body armor we wore was heavy and added to the heat we were experiencing.

The wait had just begun and I couldn't help but be worried for all these men that were there with me. They trusted my judgment and essentially were putting their lives on the line for me. This was going to be a hot and very uncomfortable stakeout.

Chapter 35

It was mid-afternoon when Blaine Alexander woke up from a much needed rest. He checked his phone and noted there were two messages.

The first was from Jake Rohn. They had located Frank's vehicle and were in the process of setting up a stakeout on it in hopes of catching Frank. Rohn said he could go to the PD and the dispatcher would have all the details.

'Dammit, this shit is getting real and I'm taking a friggin' nap!' muttered Blaine.

The second message was from Trooper Investigator Tracy letting him know they had finished recovering the body that was found and would meet him at the trooper post in Dillingham later that afternoon.

Blaine quickly got himself ready and first went to the PD to get information on the search for Frank. Upon arriving at the PD, Alexander spoke with the dispatcher, Chantra Bailey.

"Hi Chantra, exciting stuff for a newbie dispatcher."

"You're right about that; the chief said you might stop by. I can tell you what the plan was but they've been quiet for some time.

Every so often Chief Perry texts me that they are okay, but that's all I've heard," said Chantra.

"If they're watching Frank's vehicle, you won't hear anything from them until they have him or they back off. They have to maintain radio silence in order to keep their positions undetected," Blaine explained.

Chantra had a much simpler way to explain it. "So, what you're saying is they're hiding in the woods and being quiet while waiting to get the drop on Frank when he shows up?"

"Exactly!" said Blaine as he smiled at Chantra's simple, but accurate, description.

"Well, you pretty much know everything I was told. There's an ambulance standing by and my instructions are to keep it quiet while they're on this stakeout," said Chantra.

"Okay, the next time the chief contacts you let him know I'll be at the trooper post if they need anything from me. Spaulding's body has been recovered and I need to meet the investigator and crime techs there," said Blaine.

Chantra smiled as she nodded. "Sure thing Blaine."

Blaine Alexander left the PD and made the short drive to the trooper post. He went inside and found that Trooper Investigator Tracy, Trooper Jarvis and the two crime scene investigators were already there. He hated to be missing out on the capture of Frank but it seemed they had that well taken care of and besides, he had to deal with the matter of Ronald Spaulding and do what he could to assist with that investigation.

Tracy saw Blaine enter the post and nodded toward him. "There's sleeping beauty now."

Everyone looked in Blaine's direction and chuckled.

Cops just have to make fun of one another; it has to be part of the code everyone is always referring to when cops do something they don't really understand.

"Yeah, I deserved that. Is Lieutenant Rivers here?" Blaine asked.

Tracy spoke up first. "No, he's out with Rohn and the chief on the stakeout for that Frank character. They did request Trooper Jarvis and his K-9, so he's about to leave and go to their staging area on the Lake Road and be ready if necessary. The rest of us are supposed to stay here in the event we're needed."

Blaine nodded, indicating his understanding.

"Hey guys, I have to go," said Trooper Jarvis as he headed for the door.

"Okay, well let's get to this business of the recovery of Ronald Spaulding's body," said Blaine.

"Sure," said Jeff Fleener. "As soon as we find his body we can recover it."

Blaine had a confused look come across his face. "I thought the message I got from Tracy was that you had recovered his body."

"A body, but not Spaulding's body," explained Tracy.

"What do you mean by not Spaulding's body?" Blaine blurted out.

Jeff Fleener thought he could best explain the situation. "Based on my cursory examination of the body it's quite easy to determine that Ronald Spaulding was much bigger, heavier and certainly a different nationality than the body we have."

Blaine still had that look of disbelief about him. He was still trying to figure out how one person is reported missing and someone totally different is found dead and buried in the same proximity.

Fleener continued his explanation. "The body we found is likely to be that of someone who's Asian, at least fifty-five years of age and I don't believe he has been dead more than a week. We found no ID with the body or at the scene. I'm afraid I can't tell you much more until we get the body back to Anchorage for an autopsy where we can take prints and, with any luck, come up with identification that way."

You could hear a pin drop. No one knew what to say.

"So if it's not Spaulding, who the hell is it?" Blaine asked.

"I know who it is."

Everyone turned and noticed that Trooper Hill had entered the office. He was one of the troopers assigned to the Dillingham post. He'd been on an extended trip visiting villages up the Nushagak River from Dillingham and had chosen that very moment to return to the office and had overheard the last part of the conversation about Spaulding.

Tracy was skeptical. "So who is it then?"

Trooper Hill began his explanation. "On my way back to Dillingham by boat, I stopped at Portage Creek this morning. That's about thirty miles up the Nushagak River from here. I went to the village store and while I was there the owner told me about a missing person, or someone she thought may be missing."

Trooper Hill had everyone's attention. This was sounding familiar.

"His name is Chin Ho Pang and he's Korean. Apparently this is his third summer in

Alaska and he stays at a camp along the river near the village. He usually visited the village store daily while he's camping, according to the owner. The store doubles as a post office and can be described as a central location for residents and visitors to meet and catch up on the community gossip. It's been over a week since Chin has been there, or seen anywhere for that matter. I found his campsite and it looked as if no one had been there for quite some time. He likes to fish but I couldn't locate his gear. It's feared that he was off fishing and something happened to him. I have a bag containing a few personal items I found at his camp and the store owner gave me a picture taken of Chin earlier in the summer."

Trooper Hill removed the picture from his bag and handed the print of Chin to Fleener. We all gathered around and looked at the photo.

"I'd bet a month's pay that the body we dug up is that of Chin. The right age, size and nationality; it has to be him," explained Fleener.

"That would mean his body is at least forty miles or more from where he was staying," said Blaine. "This is crazy!"

Tracy was shaking his head. "The list of questions this brings to mind is at least a mile long. I need to make some notifications and get a game plan lined out right now. There's something going on here that needs to be sorted out immediately."

"I've made arrangements to have the body flown to Anchorage right away. Carlos and I are staying here for now and will be ready to work on any crime scene that may be discovered. We have evidence that needs attention and some reports to prepare," said Fleener.

Trooper Hill addressed Blaine. "Get me up to speed on this search for Spaulding; perhaps there's a connection to Chin."

Everyone began their tasks. All were thinking about how bizarre this entire situation had instantly become, but none of them could think of a single scenario in their past experiences that came close to matching this one.

Chapter 36

It was nearing 5:30 in the afternoon and the sun was lowering on the horizon. The day had inched slowly along but was reaching its conclusion. As the sun sank further in the sky and shadows began stretching to their limit, the air began cooling noticeably.

Johan Frank had spent several hours waiting for one of the floatplanes at Shannon's pond to return with Jake Rohn as a passenger. That didn't happen this day. The only thing he could think of was that Rohn had made a change of plans. Hell, if he'd been on a honeymoon in this fishing paradise, he probably would never want to return to the rat race of the city.

Time to pull the plug on this job for the time being; he had a plane to catch and he should leave right away in order to make the last flight of the day to Anchorage. His mind was made up.

Frank slowly stood and stretched his tight muscles. He stomped his feet in place in order to get the blood flowing in his aching legs. He rolled up the pad he had been laying on and then he folded up the camouflage netting he had used to help conceal his position. He stuffed his trash into the small daypack he carried and slung his rifle across his back and began the trek to his pickup that he left near the Lake Road.

As a metaphor that could easily describe his life, Frank put one foot in front of the other and plodded along steadily toward his current goal. Presently his goal was to return to his vehicle and catch a flight to Anchorage and decide how to best finish this contract and get his pay and then get on with his life.

'Keep your head asshole; you're literally and figuratively not out of the woods yet.'

It was getting late in the day. We'd been watching Frank's vehicle for more than four hours. I knew that Chief Perry was going to occasionally keep in contact with his dispatcher by text message. My mind was playing tricks on me. I had come up with countless reasons as to why Frank hadn't returned to the old pickup he left parked where he obviously felt it would go unnoticed. Most of those reasons ended with Frank flying off into the wild blue yonder and my beginning a life of constantly looking over my shoulder, wondering who was being paid to end my existence on this planet.

We used hand signals to communicate. A thumbs up to or from the chief indicated everything was good. Every time I heard the slightest sound or caught a glimpse of a bird or squirrel in the trees my heart would leap from my chest. I think I aged a year for each hour that crawled by.

Occasionally I would speak in very low tones with Lieutenant Rivers who was right next to me. He was just as anxious as I.

It was just after 5:30 in the afternoon when I heard what sounded like a twig snap somewhere in the distance to the front of me. Though I strained my eyes, I couldn't see any movement. Less than a minute later I saw the first sign of what I hoped was our prey. Looking underneath the old pickup I could see a single set of legs making their way around the back of the vehicle toward the driver's side. The legs were covered by black fatigues and black boots and they had come from the direction of Shannon's Pond. It had to be Frank I was seeing.

The plan was for everyone to follow my lead. Unless it was necessary to protect themselves or one of the team members, no one was to engage Frank before I made the first move. The object was to catch Frank by surprise and hopefully take him down with a dynamic and overwhelming first action. The idea was to take Frank alive if at all possible. There was a long line of people who wanted to ask him a few questions. I planned on being at the front of the line to find out who hired him to kill me.

Cops are always told to keep their emotions in check, to avoid becoming psychologically involved with a case; allowing themselves to become emotionally attached that way clouded their judgment and ability to make sound decisions. Screw that! This bastard killed someone I befriended; someone who was protecting me. He aimed to take my life and I wanted this monster to suffer. I didn't mean pain; I meant emotional distress – horror if I could possibly cause such a disturbing arousal in this animal. This psycho was so detached that I doubted he could feel anything physical or emotional, but I was going to try. What I was about to do wasn't in any training manual or taught in the academy or the myriad of training sessions cops attend. The team that was there with me didn't even know what I had planned. This man had to know that he'd been beaten at his own damn game.

As the black clothed figure made his way around the back of the pickup in front of me, it was obvious that I was looking at Johan Frank. His features were forever etched into my memory.

He had a rolled up pad under one arm and what looked like a camouflaged net under the other arm. He had a daypack on one shoulder and a scoped rifle slung across his back. There was a leather holster with a semi-auto pistol encased by it strapped onto his right hip.

Frank looked at ease, as if he was returning from a leisurely hike in the woods. He didn't strike me as the prepared and feared killer that his reputation had made him out to be. Some would say that a man who didn't appear dangerous was to be feared the most. He made his way to the driver door and reached to open it.

I had removed my phone from my pocket as Frank neared the driver's door of his vehicle. I pressed the call button on my phone which dialed a programmed number.

About the same instant that Frank grabbed the door handle of the vehicle and tried to open it, the phone he had in the inside pocket of his shirt, the same phone he had forgotten to dispose of, the exact phone he had taken from the room of Glenn Baxter, began to vibrate and ring. The theme tune of 'Hawaii-5-0' broke the dead silence; the ring tone on Glenn Baxter's phone could be heard not only by Frank, but by the entire team of men who had been waiting for so many hours to take this son-of-a-bitch down.

If I didn't have a rifle at the ready and trained on the chest of Johan Frank, I would've loved to have taken a picture of the look on his face as he spun around and frantically searched the woods and brush for the threat he knew was most certainly somewhere near him. It was an obvious look of knowing he was now the animal that was caught in the very trap he'd set for so many unsuspecting victims, so often in his lifetime.

Before Frank had any chance to react I was coming up out of my crouch and shouting orders as I moved toward him. Though I couldn't see them, I knew that five other men were revealing themselves to Frank as well. All with weapons trained on the killer.

"Police! Don't move! Don't - fucking - move!" I shouted orders repeatedly as I advanced toward Frank.

Frank was looking directly at me with dark and lifeless eyes. I was certain he knew I was the one he was supposed to kill, not the other way around. It was as if I could hear what he was thinking. There was this bizarre connection between us, a connection I wanted to break as fast as humanly possible. Though everything happened in a matter of seconds, it seemed as if the events played out over a twenty minute period of time.

I had hoped Frank would throw himself down on the ground with arms stretched out in front of him and screaming for us not to shoot. That's how most spineless bastards usually give up. The tougher they act, the louder they cry. That wasn't the way this man was wired. He ignored the directions I was giving him to stop, to get down on the ground and give up.

Frank started to back toward the rear of the pickup while dropping the items in his arms. His right hand shot down to the weapon on his hip and in a flash, his right arm was raised and leveling off with a pistol firmly grasped in hand and pointing directly at me as he continued to back away. Frank wasn't going to drop the gun; he wasn't about to give up as he was ordered to do. There was no other choice. I'd promised Whitney I would always come home at the end of the day and today was no different. I was ready for this; I'd played this scenario out in my head a million times. Frank had his mind made up and in doing so he had unknowingly made my mind up at the exact same instant. Frank squeezed the trigger on his handgun and a shot rang out.

I had begun to kneel at the exact instant Frank shot. The bullet whizzed harmlessly over my head. My shots were both fast and accurate. There were three perfectly round holes in Frank's chest at his heart. He was now lying on his back and staring at the sky with gun still firmly clenched in hand. His eyes were just as dark and were certainly lifeless. Johan Frank would no longer be a danger to anyone ever again.

I stood vigilant over Frank as Barry Simms moved all weapons away from the dead hit man. Chief Perry was giving directions for his men to keep watch for any potentially unknown dangers while requesting an ambulance from his dispatcher.

Lieutenant Rivers went to remove the spike strip to allow the ambulance passage to the parking area adjacent to the utility building. My knees grew weak and I fought hard to keep myself from falling to the ground and expelling the contents of my stomach.

I had just taken my first human life.

Chapter 37

It was well after 8:00 p.m. I left the scene where Frank had been shot and was at the PD. I'd already spoken to Mark Dillon and to Whitney. Naturally the feds showed up about an hour after Frank was dead. They were pretty irate that their directions not to contact Frank were disregarded. Mark told me that his response to them was: *'too damn bad, they should've made it to Dillingham sooner and they all could've kissed Frank on the mouth if that was what they wanted to do but don't even think of second guessing his men and their reaction to such a dangerous fugitive.'*

I had to laugh at Mark. He just wasn't the most politically correct fellow out there but he was a great boss, in my opinion.

The feds took over the shooting investigation of Frank. That was just fine by me; they could have it. All I cared about was finding out who hired him to come after me. I hoped they'd make good on their promise to fill us in if they made that connection.

For a cop forced to shoot someone, often the worst is the interminable waiting for the investigation. I was fortunate that the feds took responsibility for the shooting. They knew Frank, and they had brought so many agents with them to Dillingham that they wrapped up the interviews with me and the rest of the witnesses rather quickly. They didn't even seize my gun for evidence.

Now I was alone with my thoughts. Blaine Alexander stopped by a little while earlier and visited me more out of friendship than anything else. Of course he was upset with me for not physically going to get him before we set up the stakeout for Frank. I told him he was exhausted from the search he had been working on and he needed the rest.

Blaine had his plate full as well. He filled me in on the bizarre twist of finding a murder victim while they were searching for Ronald Spaulding. Blaine was pleased that since that situation had turned into a homicide, the troopers would be taking over that case at least. Now he needed to take two giant steps back and rev up the search for Ronald Spaulding again.

Chief Perry made his way into the squad room and sat down near me. "How are you doing?"

"I'm fine. Whitney was pretty upset at me at first but that was just her being anxious about all of this. Mark said I could take my time getting back to work. I want to get home and be with Whitney as soon as possible."

I could tell the chief had something more on his mind.

"What the hell was that business with the phone call to Frank? I mean, how come you didn't tell any of us?"

"Chief, you're right. I acted foolishly and it was selfish to put everyone at risk that way. To tell you the truth, I didn't want to do it but I wanted Frank to know the feeling of being had."

The chief was silent, carefully thinking of what he wanted to say. "Well, when that phone went off that way I was certainly caught by surprise. I could only imagine what Frank thought when he heard it ringing."

Chief Perry paused, letting that thought sink in. I simply nodded in agreement.

Chief Perry continued his reflection. "I really think that was a great idea to distract him. I just wish you had told someone what you were planning."

I couldn't disagree with the chief but there wasn't anything I could do to change that now.

"I'm certain that with Baxter's phone being found on Frank's body and that garrote in his bag we'll make a case against him for Baxter's death. At least that loose end is probably cleared up," said the chief.

I was tired of talking about Frank, so I changed the subject, or at least tried to. "What's your take on this body they found up at the lake? That's definitely a bizarre situation."

"I don't have a single clue about what happened in that case up at the lake, I don't think the troopers do either," said the chief.

I shifted in my chair and tugged at my collar. I think someone turned the heat up in the PD. "I can offer them my and Barry's help but right now my unit hasn't been directed to get formally involved. I just want to get back to Whitney anyway."

The chief lifted his leg and propped it up on the desk in front of him. "I spoke to Investigator Tracy and he felt that between him, Lieutenant Rivers and the other troopers that everything was covered fairly well."

We heard a door open and close and within moments Barry Simms entered the squad room and took a seat near the chief and me. "Damn Jake, those feds are pissed off at you. They had every intention to take Frank alive. I got the sense they thought it was worth it for someone else to get shot in order to have the chance to question him."

I strongly disagreed. "Well, I didn't think that way obviously. Besides, he wouldn't have been taken alive in my opinion. Look at what happened; there were six of us and he tried to make a getaway with his gun drawn and pointing it at me. Personally, I believe he wanted to die. Why didn't he fire more than the one round when he had the opportunity?"

Both Barry and the chief shrugged. They didn't know any better than I did.

"In the back of the pickup under a tarp was a gun case and suitcase that belonged to Frank. The gun case must have been for his handgun and rifle and the suitcase contained clothes and that was about it," explained Barry.

I guess talking about Frank was going to be the order of the day for a while. I suppose I should get used to that fact.

"Have you talked to Mark?" asked Barry.

"Yeah, he said I can return to Anchorage right away but would like you to stay put and keep in touch with the feds while they are here and to stay abreast of this other investigation with that body found at the lake," I said.

"Yeah, what the hell!" exclaimed Barry. "How much do you guys know about that?"

"Not much," said the chief. "The other day the troopers received a report of a missing person on the Agulowak River. Blaine was up there running the search and a body was found in a shallow grave. That was strange enough thinking their missing fisherman was found in a grave but it turns out the body is of some Korean visitor who had been camping along the Nushagak River up near Portage Creek."

"Damn," said Barry. "There aren't any roads to either place; the two locations are so far apart and isolated to boot. Any chance the Korean was at the Lake fishing or something? Crap, do you think there could be any connection to Frank?"

"No one knows at this point, but I don't see how Frank could've found his way up to Portage Creek nor did he have access to a boat to go twenty miles to the end of Aleknagik Lake. I'm sure the feds and the troopers will at least look at that possibility," I added.

Barry shook his head. "Well, I'll help in any way I can but I suppose unless our orders change I'll stay out of their way for the most part."

"I plan on catching a late flight out of here tomorrow," I said. "I'm staying the day just in case the feds need anything more from me."

Chief Perry stood up. "Look guys, it's been a long day and I have a mountain of reports to prepare, so I'm going to leave for the night and get back at it bright and early tomorrow."

Barry and I stood and shook the chief's hand.

"Okay chief, I'll see you in the morning. Thank you for everything," I said.

After the chief left us, Barry and I stayed behind and told a few war stories and laughed at a few jokes. I realized Barry was doing his best to try and get my mind off the shooting. After all he knew exactly what I was feeling.

He was off duty and standing in line at his bank early last spring when some idiot entered the bank with a shotgun and fired a round into the ceiling and demanded everyone to get down on the floor or they would be killed. Barry pulled his weapon and shot the robber in the head. Just like that; facing a man armed with a shotgun he acted without hesitation. I saw the security video and what he did was the most incredibly brave thing I'd ever seen anyone do, no doubt saving several lives in the process.

I recalled Barry telling me how his knees and back hurt too much for him to be crawling around on the floor. He was the sort of man who didn't need accolades for doing the right thing. Yeah, I thought Barry Simms was just the right person to be with at a time like this.

Marcus felt as though he had made yet another mistake. Days had passed and he hadn't heard anything from the man he hired to kill Rohn. In his eagerness and being unable to patiently wait for any news, he booked a flight to Alaska and had been in Dillingham for a few days. He had no idea why he had to be there, but he did.

His hatred for Jacob Rohn had festered and grown to the point it was obsessive and clouded his judgment and was just plain ridiculous. He was making decisions without really thinking them through, such as traveling to Alaska; there was nothing he could do in Dillingham.

It started years ago in Colorado and then continued last spring in Fort Yukon. Rohn had caused him grief and cost him money for the last time. He wanted to be certain Rohn could never interfere with his business or life again. The desire to be there when Rohn hit the ground was what he really wanted; he would've paid Jones twice the money if he could watch Rohn die.

That entire plan had been blown to shit with the death of the hit man he had hired.

He sat in his hotel room wondering what he should do next. Just by hanging around a local bar earlier in the evening he heard the rumors circulating through town about this big shootout involving the FBI and local cops with some fugitive on the ten most wanted list, and the fugitive had been killed. It didn't take a mental giant to figure out that the man he hired, Jones or whatever his name truly had been, was now dead.

A few beers and shots of cheap whiskey loosened the lips of every fisherman and cannery worker who was in the place. Now all he could think of was how he had paid out all that good money and got zero results. He was certain Rohn was still alive. Just the mere thought of Jake Rohn made his blood boil. How lucky could one person be?

Marcus needed to get the hell out of this town. *'The sooner, the better,'* he thought.

Chapter 38

Since there was no longer a threat on my life I decided to stay at a local hotel for the night. The trooper bunkhouse was somewhat at capacity with all the extra men in town and I wanted more privacy and quiet than what the transient quarters at the PD provided. I actually rested reasonably well. It turned out that I'd lied to the chief. I really didn't mean to but it was well past morning when I saw him. I had taken in a late breakfast at the restaurant and it was just past noon when I made my way to the PD.

Once inside, it seemed as if things were getting back to normal. There was one patrol officer in the squad room working on paperwork. The chief was sitting in dispatch and talking to Chantra Bailey.

Though it had been a week since Whitney and I were married, it seemed like months. I was surprisingly cheerful and thought I would spend the day around the PD and ensure there wasn't anything I could do to help out in some way.

"Hi chief, how are things?"

Chief Perry turned to face me when he heard my voice. "Good morning Jake, just talking to Chantra. Let's go back to my office."

I followed the chief into his office and he shut the door behind me. "Not much to report Jake. The feds stopped by and filled me in on what they found. All that Frank had was his weapons, a laptop and clothes plus the gun case that Simms mentioned," said the chief.

"What about Baxter's weapon and credentials?" I asked.

"They weren't found. They assume he dumped them. He had ID on him in the name of Chuck Jones so they're checking with the airlines to see if he flew under that name. In the suitcase with the clothes and laptop they found another half dozen IDs and a couple pay as you go cell phones that were most likely burn phones. They'll have to take the laptop back to their computer techs to see what they can learn from data on it. That's pretty much it," said the chief.

"It seems that Frank was ready to change his name if it became necessary. The man was a pro." I said.

"Pro or not, his business is done," said the chief.

"Do you think they're telling you everything?" I asked.

The chief sat back in his chair. "Yes I do. I believe they're over their displeasure about Frank getting killed. I suppose they realized that would've been the outcome no matter how they tried to apprehend him. I also think they'll be going out on the last flight tonight. Wait, aren't you going out on the last flight? Maybe you guys can swap recipes," laughed the chief.

"Yes, I am, and Satan himself could be on that plane and it wouldn't bother me in the least. I should be glad they agree that we did everything we possibly could in order to take Frank alive but he didn't really give us any choice. Any word about that investigation the troopers are working on?" I asked.

"No news. A couple of my officers and Barry Simms are doing some follow-up locally for them. Portage Creek and Aleknagik have been canvassed pretty well and so far they're striking out completely," explained the chief.

"Any word how the search for Ronald Spaulding is progressing?" I asked.

"Trooper Jarvis and Blaine have returned to the Chesterfield Lodge and apparently plan to re-interview everyone there. I really don't know how the search is going except that they haven't found him yet."

"This is a stone cold who done it! I wonder if there's a connection between Spaulding and this Chin Ho Pang." I thought aloud.

"From what I know, they're considering every possibility. About all they have ruled out is if Frank was involved in some way. No one rented a boat or stole one. There's no way he could have made his way to the end of the lake without a decent boat and there's absolutely no apparent motive," said the chief.

I sat there shaking my foot. I was nervous and had the bad habit of shaking my foot back and forth when I was like that. It drove Whitney nuts; she would tell me she always knew something was bothering me and something was certainly bothering me now. I just couldn't put my finger on it.

About that same moment, Blaine Alexander knocked on the chief's office door and announced himself.

"Come on in Blaine," said the chief and gestured for Blaine to enter his office and have a seat. "I thought you went back up to the Chesterfield?"

"I did, but I left Trooper Jarvis there after I got caught up on the search for Spaulding. No news there to speak of. I'm glad we didn't completely abandon the search after that body was found. I had some things I wanted to check out, so I came back to town a few hours ago. Investigator Tracy wanted me to let you guys know that he's holding a briefing about this case at 4:00 o'clock this afternoon. Jake, can you make it?" asked Blaine.

"Yeah, no problem; my flight leaves a few hours after that, so I can certainly be there," I said.

Blaine was in a hurry for some reason. "I'll probably see you then," said Blaine as he headed out the door.

I decided I would get out of there as well. "Chief, I'm going to rest up some more. If you need anything, you know where to find me."

"Sure thing, I'll see you at 4:00 o'clock," said the chief.

It was a little before 4:00 p.m. when I made my way to the trooper post. I think I was the last to show, except for Blaine, who hadn't arrived. Investigator Tracy, Lieutenant Rivers, Trooper Hill, Barry Simms, Jeff Fleener, Carlos, Officer Sharkey and Chief Perry were already seated. Trooper Jarvis was still at the Chesterfield Lodge.

"Let's get started," began Investigator Tracy. "Thanks to each of you for making it to this briefing. We have a lot to cover but please ask any questions you may have. Things have been difficult, to say the least. Some of you recently dealt with Johan Frank and the dust has barely settled on that event and now you're being asked to jump right into the strangest case I've seen in quite some time."

Tracy went on to outline everything he knew up to the minute. To be honest, there wasn't a lot to go on. A fisherman, Ronald Spaulding, had been missing from the Agulowak River for several days now. Other than his pack and fishing gear found along the riverbank, no trace of him had been located anywhere in the area. A body was found a few miles from where Spaulding had been fishing but that body turned out to be that of Chin Ho Pang. Pang had been staying at a camp several miles from where his body was discovered and it seemed that he'd been missing for up to a week. People had been questioned in Portage Creek, Aleknagik, Dillingham and the Chesterfield Lodge and nothing had been revealed that would be useful in the investigation.

After Tracy had finished his basic briefing, Barry Simms asked the first question. "Can you tell how Pang died?"

"I can answer that," said Fleener. "My best guess is that his neck was broken but an autopsy has yet to be done to confirm that."

Barry Simms had another question. "Have you found any connection between Pang and Spaulding?"

"Nothing at all," said Tracy.

Chief Perry chimed in. "Are you positive that Frank wasn't involved?"

"Good question," began Tracy. "We're fairly certain that he wasn't. We've tried coming up with a connection but it's just not there; however, we won't completely dismiss that idea."

"We invited the feds to this briefing but they're apparently getting ready to leave town and don't have the time," added Lieutenant Rivers.

It was my turn; I wanted to know how Tracy was thinking. "What do you plan to do going forward?"

"Well, I believe we should step up the search for Spaulding. I also hope the autopsy on Pang offers us some new lines of inquiry. The next thing is to do some more digging into both Spaulding's and Pang's history to make sure they haven't crossed paths somehow. Lastly, I would think we should continue interviewing as many people as possible to see if anything else turns up," explained Tracy.

I was impressed. It was clear that Tracy had already been thinking of how their time and efforts should be utilized.

There were different ideas tossed about in who to contact or what else could be done to further the investigation. The timelines for Spaulding and Pang's last known movements were there on the dry erase board for us all to see. It just didn't seem reasonable these two men had any connection or reason for their lives to have come to a similar end, assuming that Spaulding was indeed deceased.

We were just about to end our meeting and I had reluctantly decided I needed to go to the airport to check in for my flight when Blaine Alexander practically stormed into the trooper office.

"Blaine, you can get all the beauty sleep you want but it's not going to help much," chuckled Tracy.

Blaine completely ignored the attempted humor. "Everyone should listen to what I have to say. I believe I may have this figured out!"

Chapter 39

You could've heard a pin drop. All eyes were most certainly focused on Blaine and waiting for an explanation.

Lieutenant Rivers spoke up first. "Okay Blaine, tell us what you have."

Blaine crossed the room and unfolded a map of the Bristol Bay region and spread it out on the table. We all gathered around and waited for Blaine to explain what he had so boldly announced.

"The other day, Trooper Kramer from King Salmon said something to me that really didn't hit home until it was reported that another person was missing from Portage Creek," began Blaine.

"What did he say?" asked Tracy.

"He mentioned that earlier this year a fisherman was reported missing in Igiugig. The circumstances were similar to the disappearance of Spaulding and Pang. I did some research of case history in the region over the last five years and found that last year one other fisherman was reported missing in Pedro Bay and the year before that there were two fishermen who were reported missing, one from Nondalton and one from Egegik. None of these missing persons was ever found," explained Blaine as he pointed out all of these communities on the map.

"That adds up to a total of six victims in three years," said Barry Simms.

Blaine nodded and continued. "The case notes were fairly specific. All of these incidents were handled as search and rescues just as I've been doing with Spaulding. The original reports were nearly identical. These men were described as fishermen who reportedly had gone off fishing alone and simply vanished. It's common for hikers, fishermen, hunters and such to disappear in the vast Alaskan wilderness on occasion and that's how these cases were reported. There wasn't anything suspicious about any of these reports."

"No shit," said Trooper Hill. "People get lost or drown and die of exposure. It's common that their bodies are never located, especially those who aren't familiar with this country and venture out alone with little or no information left behind as to their intentions or plans."

I thought this was beginning to sound huge. "None of these cases had anything about them that raised any red flags or seemed criminal," I said.

"Except for Pang, who was found buried in a shallow grave," said Tracy.

"Exactly," said Blaine. "But remember we actually found Pang before we knew he was missing and if we hadn't come across his body that way, when the report of him being overdue was made, it would probably have been treated just like these other cases. It would've been handled as a search and rescue; just another overdue fisherman."

I was beginning to think that Blaine had made a connection with not only Pang and Spaulding but these other missing persons as well. Though it was something that had slipped past so many over the last few years, a pattern was certainly there. But these kinds of cases happened more often than you would think they should; how could anyone have caught on that it could possibly be criminal. Now I know what that odd feeling was that had been plaguing me recently. There was a murderer loose in Bristol Bay.

"I see what Blaine is telling us. Look at the map. All of the places where these men were missing from are right here in the region; six different men over the last three years. Look at the facts; men who were reportedly alone, visitors to the area and had ventured out to go fishing but never returned," I paused. "Now what does that sound like?"

"That could be the start of a victim profile, victims of a serial killer," said Blaine. "That's what I'm trying to tell everyone, as incredible as it may sound; I believe this is the work of a serial killer!"

That statement hung in the air like a bad smell. It made everyone uncomfortable. We all looked at one another with that quizzical look of *'where in the hell do we even begin?'*

Tracy spoke up. "We've already tried to connect Pang and Spaulding. I think we need to include these other victims and see how their paths may have crossed. There has to be a connection."

"Look at the map. Pedro Bay is at the tip of Lake Iliamna, about 150 miles from here. These communities are isolated; there are no connecting roads. How on earth is it possible these cases could be related?" asked the ever skeptical Barry.

"That's what I'm wondering. If there was some creepy freak floating around in a boat killing people and burying them in shallow graves, I think someone would've at least called in that they were being suspicious in some manner," declared Trooper Hill.

"Well, that's the other part of what I believe I have an answer for," Blaine said.

Once more we all turned our attention to Blaine; he had a good grasp on what this was about so it seemed logical that he had even more answers.

For a second time Blaine gestured toward the map to help explain his answer. "Barry is right; these communities are isolated.

There are no roads throughout Bristol Bay and though you could travel to every community by boat in the summer that doesn't seem feasible due to the distances involved. There are trails that can be taken in the winter but these cases all occurred in the summer so that rules out snowmachines."

"What's your point Blaine?" asked an impatient Tracy.

"The point is that the normal mode of travel to and between these communities as a general rule would be by aircraft. If there's just one person responsible for all of these missing persons, what's the common denominator? They would probably have been transported by plane to these places. The major air taxi services that fly in this region are mostly here in Dillingham but there are a couple in King Salmon and Iliamna," Blaine explained as he pointed out these locations on his map.

"Alright," said Tracy. "We need to pull flight and passenger information from all of these air taxis for the dates matching up with the missing person reports."

Blaine had paused but turned toward Tracy. "I already did that; that's what I've been up to all day. I visited the local air taxis in person and called the ones in Iliamna and King Salmon."

"What did you find out?" asked Tracy.

Blaine took a deep breath. "Well, since their records have become computerized they could easily plug in a date and retrieve schedule and passenger information for all their flights. Fortunately, their files went back several years but there wasn't a single passenger name that came up more than once on any carrier for the report dates and communities where these reports had originated. I also checked dates immediately before and after the report dates and struck out there as well."

You could tell Tracy was thinking this was a waste of time. "So, that didn't help any. What did?"

"But it did help," said Blaine.

"How?" asked Tracy.

Once again Blaine began to explain. "I decided I was looking at it all wrong. I thought it would make the most sense to look for a particular aircraft or air taxi that traveled to each of those communities about the same time that all six of these missing persons had been reported overdue. There was one charter service that fit that set of criteria for five of the six cases. None of the others even came close"

"Which one was that?" asked Tracy.

"Right here in Dillingham based at Shannon's Pond, Markey Charters," answered Blaine.

Markey Charters! My hackles went up. That was the air taxi that flew Whitney and me out to Forty Minute Lake.

"You said five of the six, which community didn't match up? Doesn't that blow your theory out of the water?" asked Tracy.

"Aleknagik," said Blaine. "There's more, not only was it Markey Charters that flew to those five other communities the very day those men went missing, but the pilot was the same for every flight. It was Bob Johnson."

Bob Johnson, I knew that name. He was our pilot!

Before anyone could speak, Blaine continued. "Markey Charters didn't have a scheduled trip to Aleknagik the day Spaulding went missing but Johnson did fly up there. Apparently he had a few hours between flights and had secured permission to land their floatplane up near the Agulowak River on the lake. They keep a small riverboat up there to use when they fly an occasional fisherman in for a daytrip. Johnson told them he wanted to do a little fishing. It was something all of the pilots did from time to time according to their dispatcher."

"I think that more than does it. We can definitely place Bob Johnson in the vicinity of all of these missing persons. We've been beating our heads against the wall trying to put this together and it makes sense now. This has to be the work of someone who has gone off the deep end. We have more than enough to go see Bob Johnson and find out what he has to say about this bizarre coincidence or at least see how he reacts if he's approached and asked some non-accusatory questions about his flights to these communities," said Lieutenant Rivers.

"So, how can we be certain it wasn't someone in a private plane that was flying around killing these fishermen?" asked Tracy.

Lieutenant Rivers had been fairly quiet as Tracy asked Blaine his questions but seemed to be tiring of Tracy's condescending tone. "I guess we can't know for sure at the moment, but I think we should start finding out by talking to Bob Johnson."

"One last thing you'll want to know," said Blaine. "Johnson should be arriving at Shannon's pond in about thirty minutes. It's his last flight of the day. I wasn't specific in my reason why I was asking for the flight information but I'd bet that as soon as Johnson walks into the office someone will tell him."

Damn, this was incredible. I needed to commend Blaine for this detective work. Even if this doesn't pan out, his intuition and thought process was commendable. I had to call Whitney as I was about to miss my flight home.

Chapter 40

We left the trooper post in two vehicles. With the recent events involving Johan Frank still fresh in everyone's mind, we thought it would be a good idea to have plenty of backup if Bob Johnson decided to make things difficult. I drove one vehicle with Barry Simms and Lieutenant Rivers as passengers. Blaine Alexander drove the second vehicle with Trooper Investigator Tracy and Trooper Hill.

The plan was for those of us in my unmarked vehicle to hang back and be available in the unlikely event we were needed. Tracy and Hill were to make the initial contact with Johnson and their goal was to return to the trooper office with him and conduct a more in depth interview if things worked out that way but at the very least they wanted to get a preliminary read on Johnson's reaction.

When suspected killers are approached, especially from cold cases, it's best that time is taken to research the suspect and have as many advantages possible. This case was somewhat different because, as Blaine had correctly surmised, Johnson was about to be tipped off to their interest and they needed to contact him before that happened to maintain the element of surprise. An early approach to Johnson was acceptable – especially since he was the only person of interest identified at this point in the investigation.

Blaine Alexander had provided Tracy and Hill with a few printouts that contained information on all the cases including dates, victim's names and locations. Criminal background and case involvement checks on Bob Johnson revealed nothing at all in his past. Johnson not having any criminal history did not lessen the chance that he could be dangerous anymore than it reduced the possibility that he was somehow involved in these disappearances, in my opinion.

Chief Perry knew Johnson and described him as a quiet man who stayed to himself and was always pleasant to talk with if you bumped into him at a restaurant, store or anywhere else for that matter. Johnson had never been in any trouble or so much as issued a traffic ticket in town according to the chief. He wasn't known to be a drinker or one to frequent the local bars. In my limited contact with Johnson he struck me as a stand up guy and excellent pilot.

As we arrived at Shannon's Pond, we saw the very same floatplane Bob Johnson had piloted when he flew us to Forty Minute Lake on short final for landing. I waited across the parking area from where the floatplanes were tethered and we expected Johnson to park the plane. Blaine's vehicle was much closer to that location and I anticipated they would wait for

Johnson to exit the aircraft and start up the bank toward the office buildings before approaching him.

It took just a few minutes for Johnson to taxi his plane close enough for him to secure it to a cleat on the dock and as expected it was Bob Johnson who exited the aircraft through the pilot's door. As soon as the plane was secured, Johnson opened the passenger doors and assisted three clients to deplane. The pilot didn't seem to notice Blaine's vehicle or give it a second look.

The passengers walked up the bank and were well out of the way. It was a good thing that they'd moved along and wouldn't interfere with contacting Johnson. After Johnson was apparently done locking down the aircraft, Tracy and Hill exited their vehicle and began the fifty to sixty yard walk toward him.

When they were perhaps thirty yards apart, I saw Tracy hold up his hand and wave to Johnson and apparently greet him. Johnson stood on the dock and waited for the two troopers to reach him.

"Hi Bob, I'm Kenny Tracy, an investigator with the Alaska State Troopers from Anchorage. This is Trooper Hill; you may know him from here in Dillingham," said Tracy as he stepped close enough to Johnson to extend his right hand.

Johnson shook Tracy's hand and also shook the hand of Trooper Hill who had also moved close enough to Johnson to make the gesture.

"Oh yeah, I know Trooper Hill from around town here. How can I help you?" asked Johnson.

Tracy expected Johnson to ask that. "Actually, I came to town to help deal with the shooting that happened yesterday. Did you hear about that?"

"I heard about it; I also heard the FBI was involved. It's all over town but you know how rumors are. How could that have anything to do with me?"

Tracy felt this was going along just fine. "It doesn't, that's practically wrapped up but I thought I would help with the search and rescue in progress up on the Agulowak River for a missing fisherman, since I had the time."

Tracy thought he saw Johnson's eyes shift when he mentioned the Agulowak.

Johnson held his composure. "Okay, how can I help?"

Tracy changed the subject. "How many flight hours do you have? I've always wanted to get my private pilot's license but just haven't found the time."

Johnson seemed to stammer a bit and seemed confused but finally answered the question. "Maybe ten thousand in all; I've been flying for years."

"That's impressive. Do you like to fish? Having access to a floatplane and flying clients to some of the best fishing spots in the world must be a great bonus; do you ever get out and do your own fishing?" asked Tracy.

"Yeah, I do my share of fishing," said Johnson.

Tracy had Johnson trying to think of a couple of different things at the same time and now was the right moment to ask a case specific question. "The Agulowak. We learned that someone saw your plane at the mouth of the Agulowak River the day that fisherman came up missing. We just wanted to know if you saw the guy. His name is Spaulding and was fishing alone. Older gentleman with white hair, and he uses a fly rod."

There was a strained silence and Johnson didn't immediately answer the question. In fact he didn't answer the question at all. Instead he quickly stepped toward Trooper Hill and pushed him backwards off of the dock and into the water. Tracy attempted to keep Hill from falling but was unable to move fast enough to be successful.

Trooper Hill was in full uniform to include a bullet proof vest, fully outfitted gun belt and boots. He was like a turtle on its back in the deep water adjacent to the dock. He was struggling to get his balance and his head remained underwater. Tracy elected to help Trooper Hill and completely ignored Johnson.

In the same motion of pushing Trooper Hill off of the dock; Johnson spun around on his heels and began to sprint toward his plane which he quickly untied and hopped on a float and pushed away from the dock. Blaine was exiting his car as I started my vehicle and began driving toward the dock.

Johnson had his own agenda, which didn't include talking to the two troopers. I was amazed how easily that man opened a door of the aircraft, jumped inside of the plane and was in the pilot seat before any of us could reach the dock. There was nothing we could do at that point. Johnson had the Dehavilland Beaver cranked and was taxiing for an apparent takeoff before anything could be done to stop him.

As we watched Johnson's plane lift off and head to the west, Lieutenant Rivers was on his cell phone talking to someone at the airport tower. Trooper Hill had made it out of the water with the help of Investigator Tracy. I could hear Hill cursing a blue streak.

"Hey guys, this is Lieutenant Rivers. I'm at Shannon's Pond and one of Markey Charters' Dehavilland Beavers just took off to the west."

The lieutenant paused. I assumed he was listening.

"Yeah it did just land but the pilot took off again. I doubt there'll be any radio contact from him but I need for you to inform me where that plane goes. The pilot is a murder suspect."

Lieutenant Rivers thanked the person he was talking to and disconnected. "That was flight services; they can get the word out and hopefully get a fix on Johnson's location. I have to call King Salmon. All the fish and wildlife aircraft and the R-44 helicopter are there and I want them to get airborne and come our way in order for us to hopefully follow Johnson or at least search for him."

"High speed airplane chase, a first for me," said Barry Simms.

"It makes a person look guilty when they run as he did," said Lieutenant Rivers.

Blaine spoke up. "I'll call the VPSO's in Manokotak and Togiak to the west. I'll tell them to be on the lookout for that aircraft. I just don't know where this guy will go."

"If it'll help, Barry and I will talk with his employer here and get some information on Johnson and find out where he has been staying. They may have an idea where he may go or how much fuel he has. They certainly will want to know Johnson has taken one of their aircraft and I would imagine they'll be eager to get it back, so I don't think cooperation should be a problem," I suggested.

Lieutenant Rivers exited my vehicle. "Good idea. The rest of us will get back to the office and start making notifications. Trooper Jarvis should be back from Aleknagik so he and Trooper Hill can get ready to go with the fish and wildlife troopers when they arrive here with aircraft; they'll need spotters. Investigator Tracy can begin a search warrant for Johnson's residence. He'll need a location and description of where he's staying."

The namesake of the air taxi, Markey himself, was at his charter business office when Barry and I arrived. After introductions, I briefly explained what was happening and that we needed some information on Johnson. Markey was more than willing to help us just as I suspected, but he was pissed as hell at us.

"Son-of-a-bitch! What in the hell were you guys thinking, letting Johnson get away with my plane? I was wondering why I heard him land and then almost immediately take off. We've tried calling him on the radio but he's ignoring us," shouted an excited Markey.

"Can I give him a try on the radio?" I asked.

"Sure," said Markey as he opened up the gate at the end of the counter and showed me their VHF radio. "This is our company channel and one of his radios should always be monitoring this channel."

I keyed the microphone and introduced myself and asked Johnson to return to Dillingham or at least talk with me on the radio. I tried this for several minutes with no results. All we heard was static and an occasional crackle over the radio speaker. It was perhaps fifteen minutes later when I heard a voice come over the radio. Markey said that was Johnson's voice.

"I'm here," replied Johnson.

"Bob, this is Jake Rohn. You took me to Forty Minute Lake a few days ago."

"Yeah Jake, you're a good man but I can't really talk right now."

"There was no reason to run like you did. That fisherman has been missing for a few days and his family is worried sick. We just want to help his family out and was thinking you might be able to help them too," said Rohn, hoping to appeal to Johnson's caring side.

"I can't be of any more help to them than they could be to me."

I knew that I wasn't getting anywhere with Johnson but I kept trying. However, he wouldn't respond. After several minutes of trying to talk Johnson into returning to

Dillingham or talking with me we heard one final radio transmission from him.

"Tell my family that I'm sorry."

That was all we heard. No amount of trying got us any further response. We obtained the rest of the information on Johnson from Markey. He described him as a quiet, dependable and honest employee. He'd worked there for about five years and lived alone in a one room cabin that was on the back side of a hangar that Markey owned.

After we had the information we needed, Barry and I thanked Markey and returned to the trooper post. We had asked Markey to let us know if Johnson came back or contacted him and he said he would. We also told Markey we would keep him posted.

"Holy shit Barry, this is the damndest thing I've ever been a part of," I said as we left Shannon's Pond.

All Barry could do was shake his head. "Me too. Who would think this type of thing would happen out in the middle of nowhere like this?"

I couldn't believe that Bob Johnson may be responsible for these deaths. Up until the moment he took off, I mean literally took off; I thought everything had to be an amazing coincidence. Just as the lieutenant said; it makes people appear guilty if they run. Bob Johnson was doing the ultimate in running.

Once we arrived at the trooper post, Barry and I went inside. Since Trooper Jarvis had returned from the Chesterfield Lodge, he and Trooper Hill had already left for the airport to meet the fish and wildlife troopers who were nearing Dillingham in their aircraft. Blaine and Lieutenant Rivers were making phone calls, so we waited until they were finished. Tracy was still busy with his search warrant and affidavit.

After Lieutenant Rivers finished his last call we filled him in on what we learned about Johnson. I told him what Johnson said on the radio.

"Any word on where Johnson is?" I asked.

"None whatsoever; I called flight services again and they had nothing to report. They have every aircraft in Alaska on alert for Johnson's plane. If someone sees it they'll call it in," explained Lieutenant Rivers.

"Markey told me that he believed Johnson's plane had at least three hours of fuel, which means he can make it as far as Anchorage or a little beyond that," I said.

"That's good to know," began Lieutenant Rivers. "I'll pass that along to flight services. I've asked the fish and wildlife troopers to begin searching lakes in the vicinity and begin eliminating places Johnson could be. They have two Cessna's, one on floats, and the helicopter, which is also on floats, to utilize in the search. I feel confident that he'll get spotted by another pilot and we'll get a lead on where he is."

Blaine Alexander came rushing into the lieutenant's office. "Flight services on line two. The coast guard just called them, there's an aircraft emergency locator transmitter signal coming from an area very close to Manokotak!"

Lieutenant Rivers quickly answered the call that was on hold. He often said yes and okay and made a couple of notes while he listened. The last thing he said before he hung up was that he had three trooper aircraft, including a helicopter that could likely get there in less than thirty minutes.

This was uncharted water for me, chasing down or tracking an aircraft this way. Everything was moving so fast but the lieutenant wasn't fazed at all. He knew who to call, what to say and how to direct resources to get the job accomplished. I thought all aircraft were followed by radar and someone could see a blip on a screen that identified their location among other details. Apparently that is for larger commercial planes and doesn't apply to smaller air taxi service or private aircraft.

"Alright, flight services received word from the coast guard of an ELT going off, the type of signal a plane gives off when it crashes. I have the coordinates which are for Acorn Peak that's next to Manokotak, about twenty miles west of here. It's an eighteen hundred foot hill. There are no aircraft in the area to check this out so I'm going to direct the trooper helicopter there right now," said Lieutenant Rivers as he exited his office and went to the radio console in the front part of the trooper post.

Within minutes, the lieutenant had provided the helicopter pilot with the information of the ELT signal and the coordinates provided by the coast guard of where the signal was coming from.

"All we can do now is wait," said Lieutenant Rivers.

Chapter 41

Marcus was making his way through airport security at the Dillingham airport. He'd decided to get the hell out of town on the last flight of the day bound for Anchorage.

He was thinking of all the time and money he'd wasted with his obsession of trying to get Jake Rohn.

'That bastard has cost me so much personal grief not to mention business and money, and has ruined my opportunity to have a stronghold in the drug trade to Alaska.'

If things weren't bad enough, there were three cops going through security and apparently would be on the same plane he would be boarding. Marcus suspected they were feds.

'Just great; now I have to share my flight with these damn assholes.'

Marcus thought it was ironic that these idiots were so close to him and occasionally one would glance at him and all he would do was smile and nod. He was far too smart for the likes of these morons. Just like Rohn, they were no match for him. They were nothing to him.

'Maybe I should just cut my losses and forget about Rohn and work on expanding my

business . . . I could buy that asshole a hundred times over.'

The main cabin door to the plane was closed a short while after Marcus boarded and took his seat. He closed his eyes and drifted off to sleep before the plane was airborne. He dreamed of choking the life out of Jacob Rohn.

In less than twenty minutes, the trooper helicopter was within sight of Acorn Peak.

Trooper Hill was the spotter in the trooper chopper and had a set of field glasses held up to his eyes. He could see smoke about halfway up the slope. As they approached the smoke, he could plainly see the wreckage of a small airplane just above the tree-line on the hill.

As they drew even closer, the binoculars were no longer needed to see that an aircraft had slammed into the side of the rock covered slope and the entire front half of the plane had burned rather intensely but was now just smoldering with very few flames present.

The helicopter pilot skillfully positioned Hill's side of the aircraft so that he could see the profile of the airplane and it was obvious there had been no survivors. The tail section of the plane was crumpled but not burned. Trooper Hill noted down the tail number of the plane and then the pilot gained altitude in order for them to have the opportunity to make radio contact with the trooper post in Dillingham.

"Trooper helo to Dillingham AST," spoke Trooper Hill into his radio headset.

"Dillingham AST, go ahead," was the response Trooper Hill heard and he believed it was Lieutenant Rivers he was talking to.

"We've arrived at an apparent aircraft crash site on Acorn Peak. The plane has burned and there's no sign of survivors. Tail number of the crashed aircraft is November-six-four-seven-six-Hotel," said Trooper Hill.

There was a brief pause over the radio but Trooper Hill heard what he thought he might. "It's confirmed that tail number is from the plane Bob Johnson left in. Can you land and get to the crash on foot to confirm if there are any survivors?"

After a brief conversation with the pilot, Trooper Hill answered. "There's a clearing at the base of the peak where we can land. It'll take at least an hour to reach the crash. We have a satellite phone we can use to reach you with once we have more information."

The trooper pilot called flight services on his radio and briefed them on what they had found and their plan to reach the plane on foot. Once that was accomplished, the pilot landed the helicopter in a clearing at the base of the hill and they readied themselves and began their ascent to the crash site.

We had been waiting at the trooper office when Trooper Hill radioed in with the information. It was confirmed; Bob Johnson had intentionally flown his plane into the side of a mountain rather than face the police. The weather was clear; there'd been plenty of visibility. It just didn't seem logical that the crash was an accident.

"Well, now we need to get to work on proving that Bob Johnson is our man or find out that he's not. It's suspected the news from Trooper Hill will confirm Johnson is deceased once he makes it to the crash site on foot. I guess I should call Markey Charters and let them know we found his plane; albeit crashed into the side of a hill," said Lieutenant Rivers.

Investigator Tracy had been working on a search warrant and affidavit which would allow the search of Johnson's residence in hopes of finding anything that would help connect him to Pang's murder as well as these other missing person cases. He finished the first draft and had printed it for us to look over. Once I read it, I made a couple of suggestions as did Barry Simms.

Lieutenant Rivers finished his call to Markey Charters and after he checked over the search warrant himself, he and Tracey went to see the DA with the document and then were planning to contact the local magistrate and get the warrant approved.

I called Mark Dillon and filled him in on the events involving Bob Johnson.

"You just as well stay there and see this through Jake. You won't get on a plane and come back to Anchorage anyway," said Mark.

"Yes I would," I said. "But I think it's too late to get on the last flight out of Dillingham."

I could see Barry suppressing a smile. He couldn't hear Mark, but he knew exactly what Mark was saying to me.

Once I ended the call with Mark, I called Whitney. I assured her I should be back to Anchorage the following day. She told me she loved me but knew the chances were that something would come up and I would get delayed even longer.

After I was finished speaking with Whitney I stood up. "Let's go Barry; I'll buy dinner. Where did Blaine go?"

"He decided to go with Tracy and the lieutenant. He wanted to help search Johnson's place," said Barry.

"He should be there. I'd bet money that they link Johnson to all of these cases and Blaine is the one to thank for that," I said.

Barry and I had a great dinner, the most relaxed I'd been for several days now. We took our time and talked about everything under the sun. Just as we were finishing up our leisurely meal, I received a text from Blaine. He said they were concluding their search of Johnson's place and wanted to meet us at the trooper post. I paid the bill and we left the restaurant.

We'd been waiting at the trooper post about ten minutes when Lieutenant Rivers, Investigator Tracy and Blaine arrived. We all met inside the lieutenant's office.

"How did the search go?" I asked.

"Trooper Hill called me a short while ago. He made it to the plane and verified there was one charred body in the wreckage, in the pilot's seat, and was most certainly Bob Johnson," was the lieutenant's answer to a different question than I had asked.

After taking a seat at his desk, Lieutenant Rivers reached into a canvas tote and pulled out a journal, some maps and a small leather change purse-like object. "This is all we found."

I wasn't sure how those things related to the case but waited for an explanation.

Lieutenant Rivers unfolded a map that was of the Bristol Bay region and a second map of the Bethel region which was to the north and west of Bristol Bay. The maps were clean and in decent condition but the one of Bristol Bay had six red circles and six blue dots on it and the one from Bethel had three red circles and three blue dots.

The lieutenant began his explanation; it was just what I expected. The six red circles on the Bristol Bay map corresponded with the communities where the reports of the six missing persons originated. "Look at these blue dots on this map. I can't speak for all six, but the one here at the end of Aleknagik Lake seems to be in about the exact position where Pang's body was found."

If that was the case, then the remaining five blue dots represented shallow graves where the other missing persons could be found. After all, the dots were reasonably close to where the fishermen were reported to have gone missing.

"That's just the beginning," began Tracy as he pointed at the journal. "The writings in this journal began about ten years ago. We can assume this is Johnson's own writing but I believe we can find enough samples to have an accurate comparison done. They are the writings of a disturbed person. It appears that Johnson's wife left him and he was never able to get over it."

"That's right; I spoke to Johnson when he flew us out to that cabin. He told me about a bad divorce ten years ago and he then moved to Alaska," I recalled.

"Get this," said Tracy. "His wife left him for some guy who was on the Bass Master fishing tour – a professional fisherman according to the journal. These were ramblings on how he hated fishermen and some of the dates when he wrote of doing dark things definitely correspond with the dates of these missing persons. The entire journal has not been read, but I bet we'll find a confession in this."

We were stunned. How in the hell could this be so complicated but turn out to be so simple?

"Oh but wait; there's more," said Blaine.

With a flair for dramatics, Blaine held up the small leather purse and pointed at it. "The final piece is in this leather change purse. There are nine fishing licenses in here – six belong to the six missing persons that I told everyone about earlier, including Pang and Spaulding. I'll bet the other three will belong to the blue and red marks on the Bethel map. Johnson was keeping trophies!"

Barry and I looked at one another in disbelief. This was unreal.

I sat and listened to the excited talk of these men for more than an hour. This past week had taken a lot out of us all. Chief Perry was able to break free from his work and came over to sit in on the bull session that had been going on for quite some time.

This was always an important time in a cop's life. After traumatic events such as these, such impromptu and informal debriefings did more to relieve stress than anything you could plan and require these men to participate in.

The range of emotions that I was feeling was indescribable. I was married, targeted for murder, killed a man and had a hand in the investigation of what turned out to be a serial murder – in just one week's time. I needed a drink, but most of all I needed my wife. It was late, I was tired and I had some travel arrangements to make.

I stood up and shook everyone's hand. "Guys, this has been – well, I'm not sure how to best describe it, but I'm glad everyone's safe and even happier this guy won't kill anyone else. I have a bride at home waiting for me and I need to make plans and get the hell out of here as fast as I can before she divorces me."

I started for the door and over my shoulder called out my parting words. "No offense guys, but I prefer to spend time with her!"

Before I could make it out the door I heard Blaine call out to me. "Hey Jake!"

I turned to face him.

"None taken," said Blaine with a smile.

Chapter 42

I sat alone in my living room; well, I wasn't completely alone. My faithful mutt Archie was at my side. Whitney was at work; she had landed a job as the business manager for a company that owned three hotels in Anchorage.

It had been almost two months since Whitney and I had been married and that mess in Dillingham had gone down. Though it was Friday, I had taken the day off work to just sit at home and catch up on some of my favorite TV programs that were waiting on the DVR.

At about 3:30 in the afternoon the doorbell rang and upon answering it, I saw Mark Dillon standing there holding a packet of papers.

"Hi Mark, did you miss me?"

"Not at all, but I thought you might want to see some of this," Mark said as he made his way inside and then handed me the papers which were contained in a folder embossed with the U.S. Justice Department logo on the front.

I looked at the quarter inch thick stack of papers as if it was nothing more than dreaded homework that I would simply toss onto the table and probably forget about.

"I can give you the low down if you prefer," said Mark.

"I prefer," I said.

"For starters, the report on the DNA collected at the crime scene where Baxter was killed matches the DNA from Johan Frank. He had Baxter's phone and the murder weapon matched."

"Not surprised," I said wryly.

"That's the best news I guess. Frank was certainly responsible for Baxter's murder, but there's nothing more in the report that you would really care to hear . . . well, except they did say the shooting of Frank was justified," said Mark.

I didn't even care to respond to what they thought; I was there and knew it was justified but I suppose I was happy that a bunch of paper shufflers from Washington D.C. agreed.

"Frank had several reservations on flights departing Dillingham the day he was killed. He used different names that matched the identifications found in his belongings to make those reservations," added Mark.

"Anything about who hired Frank or what may have been on his laptop?" I asked.

"Nothing about who hired him; that was a dead end according to the report. There were some redacted portions concerning the laptop but I was assured there was nothing found that would help identify his employer," explained Mark.

"We know it was Marcus, but dammit, who the hell is this Marcus?" I asked.

"Jake, we haven't been able to make any progress as to his identity. Not here, not in Colorado. This guy is a ghost."

I know that my expression was blank. I've agonized over that very subject. Who in the hell was this guy and why in God's name would he be so dead set to have me killed? I just haven't found any answers to these questions.

"What have you heard regarding the investigation on the Bob Johnson case in Dillingham?" asked Mark.

"Blaine Alexander called me earlier this week. It seems that there were three missing person cases in the Bethel area that have been linked to Johnson in addition to the six in Bristol Bay. They've been able to locate a total of seven of the nine victims in shallow graves. They all were killed in the same manner; each had a broken neck. The case is solid enough to close each death as a homicide with Bob Johnson as the perp," I said.

"There was quite a lot happening at the same time, it's great that everything worked out," said Mark.

"You're telling me!"

"Okay Jake, I'll see you Monday?"

"Yeah, I'll be there. See you then," I said as Mark left Archie and me alone with my thoughts.

#############

Notes from the Author

I certainly enjoyed writing Deep Lies and felt the story has not only become broader but I've introduced a few characters that I'd like to expand upon in other books.

Once again, I've drawn upon my time as an Alaska State Trooper while stationed in Dillingham, Alaska, to help with this story. The four years I spent as the Bristol Bay Area Post Commander were among my favorite years as a Trooper. The communities, culture, untamed wilderness and people all were a positive influence not only to me but to my family as well.

While I was stationed in Dillingham, a fellow Trooper and friend that was an academy roommate of mine was killed in the line of duty in another part of the state. I've never forgotten this man and don't believe I ever will. I made a reference to him in this story in a way that I'll be the only one to recognize – but it's there. He was someone that was special and we shared so much during our time at the academy. Many of you will understand exactly what I mean by this. Though he and I went our separate ways after the academy and never again worked together, we were always friends. His work and ultimate sacrifice is an inspiration.

There are other references and characters in this story that relate to things I'd heard or people that I worked with over the years. The VPSO (Village Public Safety Officer), Blaine, is based on one of Alaska's best VPSOs who still works in the Bristol Bay region.

For me, writing goes beyond telling a story, it's brought to life by my experiences as an Alaska State Trooper - even in a fictional tale. Thank you for reading Deep Lies and look for Clear Lies, the next book in the 'Lies' series that I believe will answer many questions you may be asking yourself about Jake Rohn and his past.

Sincerely,

R. A. Quinn

About The Author

After nearly thirty-five years in Alaska, R. A. Quinn now resides in Pueblo, Colorado. A recent move to Colorado where his wife was raised and has several family members, who have made him, and his family, feel at home. It has been a positive and exciting time. The much warmer weather and wide open roads are perfect for riding motorcycles.

At the moment Quinn is writing and enjoying life which has included much more traveling and visiting family across the U.S.

Contacts for R. A. Quinn; feedback is encouraged:

raqo49@gmail.com   email R. A. Quinn

@BooksByRAquinn   follow R. A. Quinn on twitter

www.facebook.com/booksbyraquinn
to follow R. A. Quinn on facebook for information on upcoming books and contests

Titles by R. A. Quinn

Frozen Lies (1st Jacob Rohn Novel)

Deep Lies (2nd Jacob Rohn Novel)

Available from Amazon and Barnes & Noble.

Coming soon, *Clear Lies,* book 3 in the Jacob Rohn Series. This will be the 3rd and final book in the 'Lies' trilogy. *Clear Lies* will reveal the questions everyone has asked about Rohn's past and will be a must read.

About the Front Cover

The cover of Deep Lies was designed by R. A. Quinn. The photo is of Aleknagik Lake which the author took on one of many fishing trips there.

The lake is 350 feet deep in places and is clear and cold.

Alaska is a beautiful place. Aleknagik Lake holds a special beauty as well as fond memories for the author.

Thank you once again for reading *Deep Lies*.